AIDAN M...

Aidan Mathews was born in 1956 in Dublin. He was educated by the Jesuit Fathers before attending University College, Dublin, Trinity College, Dublin, and Stanford University, California. His published work includes two selections of poetry, *Windfalls* and *Minding Ruth*, and three plays: *The Diamond Body*, which has been produced in Dublin, London, Boston, Avignon and Paris; *The Antigone*, an absurdist re-working of the original text; and *Exit/Entrance*, a surrealist play about a suicide love pact. He has received a number of prizes, including the Irish Times Award in 1974, the Patrick Kavanagh Award in 1976, the Macauley Fellowship in 1978–9 and an Academy of American Poets Award in 1982. He is at present a radio drama producer with RTE, living with his wife and daughter just outside Dublin.

Aidan Mathews

ADVENTURES IN A
BATHYSCOPE

First published in Great Britain in 1988 by Martin Secker & Warburg Ltd.

Sceptre edition 1990

Sceptre is an imprint of Hodder and Stoughton Paperbacks, a division of Hodder and Stoughton Ltd.

British Library C.I.P.

Mathews, Aidan Carl, *1956–*
 Adventures in a bathyscope.
 I. Title
 823′.914 [F]

ISBN 0-340-50800-0

Printed and bound in Great Britain for Hodder and Stoughton Paperbacks, a division of Hodder and Stoughton Ltd., Mill Road, Dunton Green, Sevenoaks, Kent TN13 2YA. (Editorial Office: 47 Bedford Square, London WC1B 3DP) by Richard Clay Ltd., Bungay, Suffolk.

Some of these stories have appeared
in the following publications:

Stand, Irish Press, Irish Times
Irish Living Voices (Rainbow),
Best Short Stories 1987 (Heinemann)

Others have been broadcast
on RTE and BBC 3.

CONTENTS

for Trish who knows why

SCHOLASTICS

WHEN I think of him now, I remember his hands. This too is strange: at the beginning, I was fascinated by his face. He stood at the window, that first night, taking off his soutane; I watched him closely. When he frowned, the skin puckered between his eyes where his eyebrows met, but nowhere else. One of his eyebrows was fair, and the other was brown. I think also that he had forgotten to shave under his lip, I am not quite sure; there was a darkness though. How many years later, I was in the foyer of a theatre, and I found myself staring at a head by Epstein, an anguished face full of laughter. I was with people at the time, but I heard myself saying: of course.

Yet now I think more often of his hands. When he spoke, he would swerve them with the deftness of a woman parting fibres of wool. I used to watch them as if, at any moment, they might release small birds, or a bird's egg. The first time I was in his room, he gave me orangeade. He poured it with that same quick elegance into a glass, a tumbler that smelled of toothpaste. It was sad, perhaps; the sadness had no proper name. I took it as though he were telling me a secret.

'Are you happy at home?' he asked me.

'I don't know. I suppose so. It's hard to tell what you feel when you've always felt the same thing.'

'You'll fall in love some day,' he said. 'At least, I imagine you will, and it may be for the best. You won't sleep. You might even lose weight. And you'll realize, I don't know, that up until then you've been unhappy.'

'Yes,' I said, looking at his hands. Under me, under the bedspread with its brown, stitched roses, a bed-spring croaked.

'Nothing matters very much,' he said, and his hands flinched upward through the blue shadows seeping out of the carpet. 'Yet everything has a certain importance.' He said the word Everything as if it were two words, and not one. Outside, I heard a bicycle bell and a car door slamming, and three voices talking about shoes.

'What I want to know,' I said, 'is why Jesus didn't tell them about penicillin.'

'What do you mean?'

'I mean it would have helped everyone if he'd told them. He must have known, and about electricity too. If we'd had electricity then, where would we be now? Just think.'

'I don't know,' he replied. 'What I want to know is why he bothered to tell them at all.'

'About what?' I asked.

'We were getting on well enough. Then along he strolls to persuade us that, secretly, everybody is unhappy.'

His face was different when he said these things, it altered subtly. It was strange, like the smell from other people's kitchens. I wanted him to put on the other face, the look like that of parents waiting at a station barrier as a train draws in. I had seen it twice before; it had a privacy I wanted to protect. But he stood swiftly, and strode from the window. Light tore at his shoulder.

'Let's have a bearfight,' he said.

We clutched and grappled, swaying among the blue and the yellow outbursts of sun, knocking over the prayer stool, a high pillar of books. Afterwards I fell back on the bed, help-less, hearing my heart make curt, wooden sounds like spoons on tables. He lay above me. He pinioned me and tickled my armpits.

'You are weak,' he told me. 'There are seven days in the week, and you are weak.' That was a thing we always said to each other after our bearfights.

I watched the ceiling shift. I could smell smoke on his shirt: it was one of his odours. But he prised himself loose, walked over to the basin, and stooped to the tap. When he turned, his nose and his jaw were wet. A drop ran down his neck, and soaked into his white shirt. It made a grey stain.

'I hate to smell like a priest,' he said.

He took us both for English and for Latin. I was appointed Keeper of the Blackboard, the one boy permitted to be out of his place. Often, when I had cleaned it, he would sketch cartoons in many colours, so that his fingers became soiled with pink and red and purple chalk like a primitive, daubed African. Then he would clean them, one by one, on the wings of his soutane until his hands were again a white movement, a slow waver and rush. Once, in the church at lunch-break, I found a fresh green stripe smeared on the back of a bench. I knew he had been there, and might still be there. I did not rub out the green mark; I left the church quickly.

Later that afternoon, he let me leaf through the large book from which he read stories. It was bound in red morocco, like the gospel on the lectern; the print was a bold black with vivid capitals at the start of each chapter. I turned the pages at the corner. He was leaning above me: the back of my head brushed the lapel of his jacket; we were too near, I know that, now. He put his hands on the desk-lid, at the sides of the book: the odour of the paper was like slips, silk slips in a hot-press. He pointed to a picture of Greek fighting men, two soldiers crouched in combat, one with a drawn sword, the other with a poised spear. They were Paris and Menelaus: the first was a coward, his opponent a hero. A hero cast scorn on cowards, but cowards were cleverer, there were more of them. And my world grew larger, its edges pushed out, painfully.

He could be stern too. Once, he returned an essay I had written, with the words:

'What was the title of the theme I set?'

'Xmas or Christmas.' I was prompt, I had not forgotten.

'Fine. That's a question, isn't it? It may not find an answer, but it must provoke an argument. Don't you see?'

'Yes.' He did not smell of smoke from cigarettes when he walked into the classroom; he had to stand at the window beside his prayer stool until the sun warmed him, before the smell came out of him, like scorched grass in a garden.

'Here, you see, you use the same construction too often, you repeat yourself, you fatigue the reader: and then, and then, and then. It isn't sufficient to relate a story. You must try to persuade me that your point of view is both important and sensible; you must train yourself to be cautious with words, or a word. A word is a precision instrument, it does many things, it declares war, it signs a treaty of peace. Also, you should remember to include such words as: but, however, still, nonetheless, moreover. And perhaps. Will you do that for me?'

'Perhaps,' I said.

I waited for him each evening at five o'clock, at lighting-up time. He would step out from the rhododendrons beside the bicycle shed near the bomb shelter where the practice nets were stored. He wore, always, a yellow balaclava. Once, he

came without it, he stepped out from the rhododendrons: it
was not the same. I went home early.

I forgave him of course, but I was put out. For the first time,
he had not closed the circle: our moment together was not
complete, the risk went out of it. Still, his room included
me again on the next night. He arched his back at the window,
the breadth of his shoulder blacked out the window spaces.
How he restored the room to its own shape, a warm curve
around him, upright, between the ledge and the prayer stool!
Once, I had sat there by myself. The place was angular. Other
bodies had slept in it before him; other scholastics would
distress it, after his departure. Now, he held up the tumbler
to the light; his hand revolved it, checking for flaws. Then he
filled it with orangeade and with water. The smell was coming
out of him, of cigarettes, his smell.

'You always think the glass is chipped,' I said, happily.

'Have you any new words?' he answered.

'Magnanimous, acknowledge, hilarity.'

'Are you sure you understand them?' he urged. I preferred
the way in which he said Understand; it was a brown word,
like thistle. 'Put them in sentences,' he demanded.

'The man was magnanimous. He acknowledged he had not
been mistaken. This met with much hilarity.'

'Good. That's quite right.' He took out of his drawer a
cutting from a newspaper, and plucked a fountain pen from
the pocket of his jacket. 'You can help me with this,' he told
me. 'It's a competition, run by a firm that produces foot
powder. I use it myself, in fact, after matches; prevents
athlete's foot, quite good stuff. You have to concoct a slogan
for an advertising campaign to promote walking. The prize is
a car.' His hand capered and delved, it made a sign like the
figure two in the air.

'What do we need a car for?'

'For a fast getaway,' he replied, in an accent that was American, sharp.

'Where would we travel to?' I pressed on the sag in the centre of the bed, to hear the spring wheeze. His fingers curled, like fern, or a tendril bending toward light.

'Venezuela!' he cried out.

'Afghanistan!' I shouted; I ate the colours of its word.

'Listen!' he insisted. He was loud now, his hand reaching up to haul down the air, like stones. 'Listen! Tierra del Fuego.'

He spoke it like a password, softly; it was not addressed to me, I overheard him. I said, awkwardly:

'The Holy Land.'

His face withdrew into its features; he was not waiting at a station like a parent.

'Why in God's name do you think of the Holy Land?' he said. It was less a question than a reprimand, it had no stress of asking.

'It was called Palestine then.' I was upset, I spoke hurriedly. 'God promised it to the people, Moses led them there. He made the water spurt out of the stone, but he never reached Palestine, himself.' It had belonged to me the day before, the word for the Holy Land when Moses wanted to bring his people there; it had been brown, with some green in it, a hint of wind on the blades of a palm tree. Now, the colours had gone out of it.

'I forgot,' he said. 'You're being prepared, for confirmation. It's your course work. I'm sorry.' His hand parted, it cupped water, it let the water trickle. 'Do you think much about being confirmed? Are you anxious? Have you problems, a problem?'

'Do I have to wear a rosette? I hate them, they're desperate yokes.' I was glad again, the room curved round us, a cloak twirling.

His face broke out with gaiety. 'You're gas,' he said. 'What name are you giving yourself?'

'Thomas.' I pronounced it as Germans do; it was sterner.

'After the Apostle, the one who doubted, doubting Thomas?' He said it the way the Gospel does. His face darted out, there was a train approaching, I smelled cigarettes; his hand stirred like a Thai dancer's.

'No,' I told him. 'Try again.' I sat back in the sag on the bed, and pressed. The circle was closing, it took me in, like arms.

'Thomas Aquinas?'

'No. Guess again.' It had closed, was perfect, a palindrome.

'Thomas A'Becket? Is that it? Is that the right reason?'

'Thomas More.' I gave in. 'I saw the film on Sunday.' His hand closed on itself, as if it held a pebble, a small stone.

'Are you pleased?' I asked. 'I did it to please you.'

He crouched across his lap, like a foetus, curling. In his left hand, he clutched a cigarette: its smoke made a crooked flex around his knee and wrist. He looked up. His eye twitched; it was moist from the smoke of his cigarette.

'I love you,' he said. He straightened himself, and punched the cigarette, rapidly, against the brick facing on the fireplace.

'Time for a bearfight,' he said.

That was when first I felt the need, it was a need, to give him something, by way of proof or gesture. I may even have understood how much it cost him to speak those words, with his tongue and his throat and his breath. He had to be told, in his turn, that I would labour to earn them, the three sounds he had risked in the air, and could not now take down or put

back. They were spoken, were stones, made of circles and
curves, the substance of our silences.

I made out lists, and then a short list. I dithered for a while
over a porcelain statuette I found in a pawn shop on the
quays, a green and grinning Buddha with three chins. It had
not been mine though, from the start: it remembered other
hands, the touch of an owner who might wish, often, to be
restored to it. Later, I saw a tea service, set on a metal salver
like a paten, in a shop that sold table-ware. But it was not
marked: it was too elegant.

I decided to make my own gift. I wanted to construct a
ship, a model of a man o' war. I would piece it together out
of bits and remnants, warm, dented things. I set to, with – it
was his word, he had spoken it for me – with alacrity; but it
came to grief. I had amassed materials: papier mâché, crêpe
paper, sticks and slates: the heap fought to become a shape,
and flagged. I was ashamed. I put aside the plasticine and
gum. My father, standing over me, sighed.

'Things cannot hold,' he said, as if he were repeating the
refrain to a prayer, as if he were intoning. 'The centre falls
apart.'

I did not understand my father's intoning, he did not mean
cloaks twirling, or a train coming in.

'Always, when my father comes home, he stands at the fire,
and I feel uncomfortable.'

His eyes asked: Why?

'Always,' I replied. 'I prefer it in class where I sit at the
back beside the radiator, but not because it's hot.'

Softly, the room spoke: Why?

'You can think what you like. When people stand behind
you, they know, or they seem to know. It's like going to bed.

When I get into bed, I sleep with the wall behind me, and I dream better.'

The world of the room hummed, like bees.

I bought a large assembly kit, a scale copy of Lord Nelson's *Victory*. It comprised two hundred segments; the manual of instructions was seven pages in length. It would take two months, at an hour an evening, to stitch it, to rig and pamper it. I hoped, fiercely, to complete it for his ordination. I would present it privately; better, I would leave it on the mantelpiece in his bedroom, beside the photograph of the lady with the blue hair-clip. At the end of the day, he would return, tiredly, to be astonished by it. He would be elated. He would know.

I worked on it, each evening, at the tall table in the study. After minutes or a half hour, the small of my back smarted: I kept on; I put the goad of the small of my back into the parts of the boat, the jib boom, the galley window panes. It was a risk, inserting sections, like the syntax of a Latin sentence. I had to be sure of the connections. Also, I had never handled such delicate pieces: my grasp was not trained.

Still, I looked forward to the evenings; they gave my day a tendency, a finishing tape. Always I had one ear cocked attentively for the buzz from the bulb in the desk-lamp, like a damaged insect flapping on glass; that was a sound I liked. Or my mother knitting, the brisk swish of her needles as she tacked and topstitched. Once, she stole up, quietly, behind me, to where I sat. She leaned over me, I could smell the breath of her mouth on my ear. She studied the model, closely. I knew she was glad because she hunched with a gesture like a coax, her breasts flattened against my shoulder-blades. I looked at the ship too. I had lashed the bowsprit, stepped the mizzen-mast on the poop deck, and slotted the cannon into their embrasures. It was taking shape, unfolding like a fox-glove or a hand in greeting. My mother hugged me, briefly.

'You'll choose your wife with care,' she said.

But my father was brusque. He came in, at the stroke of nine, to watch the news. He stood at the scuttle, listening to the bulletin. Then he said to the television:

'The working classes are having a field day.'

As he left, he glanced down at me. I had begun to daub the hull-plates with a copper varnish: the tips of my fingers glistened with ooze. I stared up into his glance. The bridge of his nose had two pinch marks, like a tooth-bite, from the grip of the glasses that he read with. His smile tried.

'That won't get you into college, you know,' he said.

'My father has pinch marks on his nose, just like you.' The bed-springs wheezed and shuffled. The room drew down around us like an old rug. His hand made oranges, and tossed them.

'Is that a fact?' he said.

'Yes!' I shouted. I was soothed; I sensed the tug of his mood. He levered himself, lightly, from the polished floor, and gathered up his prayer mat in long, loose folds like a parchment scroll.

'Do you know,' he began, 'I should loan you my copy of the *Oxford Dictionary of Quotations*. It would greatly improve your conversation. Everybody would regard you as a prodigy. I could sell you to a circus, or a chat show.'

'Your proposal,' I replied, 'is most uncongenital.'

He whooped, and his head tilted to field a ball. 'You're priceless,' he said. 'You remind me of something I read this morning. A parliamentary report, no less, by some madman. "After a lengthy sitting," this genius says, "the motion was passed and the issue dropped." I ask you, can you cap that?'

'Priceless!' I answered, watching his hand. It drew down the cord of a blind, or dealt cards. The wall of the room slid forward and inward, like a low cave-face, slack canvas filling.

'What happened,' I asked, 'about the slogan?'

'We were late for that,' he said, sadly. 'We missed the closing date.'

'Never mind.' I tried to soothe him. 'We can enter another one, sometime.'

'Yes,' he said, 'You know, I've been filling application forms for twenty years. I do it in my sleep. I see pink sheets with perforations and dotted lines. They pounce on me from every corner, shrieking – Fill us up! In block capitals!'

'I had to get so many kinds of documents, and things, for my confirmation, you've no idea,' I explained. 'My birth certificate, even, was a different colour. Must you do that for your ordination?'

'No,' he said, shortly. He lit a cigarette and exhaled the smoke in a cone over the blotting paper on his desk. It was odd that, at times, the cigarettes he lit did not smell of him. He laughed: almost a grunt.

'I imagine Jesus,' he said, 'I imagine Jesus. Saying to Peter: "What was your father's occupation, and your mother's name before marriage?"' His fingers snapped a knife shut. I jabbed the scoop in the bed, and it gave out, tiredly.

'Tell me,' I said, 'when it happens.'

'What?'

'When Jesus goes into the host, I mean, after you speak the words. Does the host get lighter then, or is it heavier? What word makes him turn the bread into himself? Is it when the priest says Corpus, or does it start with Hic?'

His hands pressed a melodeon, and met; his fingers touched. He stepped to the window, and peered out, as if he had heard someone calling him. I listened too: I heard the whoosh of a racquet and a struck ball flump in netting. He cocked his head in the poor light; a draught stirred the crease of his hair. Sunlight struggled from cloud, it lunged through the panes, a fist that struck the skin of his face. There was a red bruise of sun on his cheek! But the cloud fought back, the sun went out, the burn paled. He pitched his cigarette in the stone grate.

'I can't tell you that,' he said. 'It's a secret.'

'I understand. It doesn't matter.' The light strengthened and became violent, like a bright sky through stained glass. His face was hidden in vividness, a density of blue: my eyes stung. I wanted the moment to be over; I could not endure it. He might have asked me anything as he stood there with the light cascading, a higgledy stocking of wheat. I would have confessed some terrible fiction or invented sins to be forgiven by him. But the room broke down beneath its weight of light and smells that were his. He stretched at the bookcase and plucked a paperback from the second shelf. Hurriedly, he thumbed through it.

'I read your poems,' he said. 'I liked the last but one, "The Crash On My Road". It stood out, it was precise. You must learn, now, about rhythm, which is more difficult. Listen.' He held off the book at arm's length and he read: '"They say I was sent back from Salamanca, and failed in logic . . ." Aren't they lovely, those lines? Some day, perhaps, you may come to make up a poem like that. It takes time, though, and skill. You have to wait; the waiting is part of the poem.'

I said the words a second time for him, in his voice, an intoning. 'Pestle,' I suggested, tasting it, 'is a nice word, and so is alabaster. I think they are, anyway.'

'Do you know,' he said, excitedly, 'your voice is breaking. You're getting on. You're growing older.' He tapped the book against my forehead, and stared up at the ceiling. 'Do you know,' he continued, 'this will have been the year when your voice broke. Imagine.'

He swung his arm and squeezed the book into its place, between a rank of Penguins and a squat Bible. I watched him press his face to his wrist.

'Does each image count?' he said into his wrist. 'Must I add them all up?'

I finished the *Victory*, and I brought it to him. I had meant to wait until the day, but my patience failed. I put it among straw in a small crate that had held oranges: Hebrew letters were printed on the sides of the box, and the English word, Fragile, on the lid. When I carried it into the room and set it on the bed, it leaned in the sag. I heard the model slide, and the straw tinkle. He hunkered beside it and forced the top, gently.

'What have we here?' he kept saying. 'What have we here?'

'Guess,' I said.

'St Anselm's halo,' he wondered, 'complete with a three-prong double adaptor?'

'No!' I pounded his shoulder, delightedly.

'A seventeenth-century miniature ploughshare from a Swiss canton?'

'Stupid!'

'The left trouser leg of Eirik the Red?'

'Idiot!'

But the box was open, the smell of the straw seeped out, and the odour of varnish. He eased his hands among the wisps, and picked out the model. Blades of straw dangled from the rigging. He blew them off, one by one, and raised the boat high, like a priest lifting a chalice.

'I don't deserve this,' he said. 'I just don't deserve this, you know.'

'It's for you,' I said. 'I made it for you. It's for your ordination.' He ducked his head, and the ship slipped, giddily, between his fingers. But he held it, grasped it, the masts minutely shaking. He settled it on the desk and probed it with a biro. He was intent, absorbed now.

'It's quite perfect,' he decided. 'It's like one of those ships in bottles, in an English pub. I'll treasure it, have no doubt of that. Believe me. I can only say: thank you.'

He crouched beside me, and placed his hands on my knees.

'I'll keep it on the mantelpiece,' he told me, 'beside the lady's photograph. Now I want you to listen to me for a few moments, and I want you to understand, or to try to understand, what I'm going to say.' He spoke in a sober way at first; then in a light tone, as if it were a small thing, a match cancelled.

'I'm not being ordained this year. I'm too young, you see.' His voice quickened, he saw my consternation. 'I'm too young,' he insisted. 'It's a terrible disappointment, for me too. The problem is, you see, it has to do with age; it's like being kept back a class, because of your birthday.' His grip tightened on my kneecap, the blood ran from his hand, and made it white. 'Please,' he implored, 'don't make it worse for me. You don't know what I'm feeling.'

He would not wear his new words, alb and chasuble and stole. I would not serve his second mass, receive his second blessing. I sat stock-still, aghast. Then I scrutinized his hands. There was a mark on his finger, where he had taken off his ring. I wondered where the ring was. I said:

'I'll be late for dinner.'

My hands were cold on the bars of my bicycle, because I had no rubber hand-grips. I heard, somewhere, the whirr of my chain, as I freewheeled down the avenue. We would meet, talk; I might even visit his room for orangeade and windows.

But it would not be the same. The smells had gone out as he spoke, like a fire you put earth on.

Near the kerb, at the crossing, a ruffled chaffinch waded in a puddle, furiously pecking its reflection.

For three weeks, I avoided him. Then, on a Friday, I spied him in the sacristy, tucking green vestments. His sandals smacked the floor, with a sound like libraries. I could not help myself. I went in. When he saw me, his face stirred, like particles of dust in a sun-trap small winds tease.

'Bring me bread and wine,' he said, softly.

I brought them to him, the hosts and the cruets.

Summer broke loose and ran amok, a pack of travelling players. All through the thick evenings, the voices of children spread like wine stains on a table-cloth. Often, I walked the perimeter path, from the pavilion to the swings in the park. It was quiet there. I met perhaps a priest with a hat on and a book in his hands who never looked up; or two, with walking sticks, striking at nettles. I liked to be there. I used to scuffle the grit: the sound pleased me, of gravel displaced.

When last we met, we set off down the path, together. I had stayed on, that day, after the school closed: I wanted to practise in the nets by myself. When I reached them, he was there, in a tight tracksuit, bowling. He ran with short strides to the mouth of the net, and hurled the ball, swiftly, down the length of the crease. The ball bounced high, it spun to the bars, then trickled to the slack coils at the base of the netting. He retrieved it, and walked back to bowl again, rubbing the ball on his thigh. I watched him for some minutes. When he homed on the line of the crease, his shoulders hunched; but, as he threw it, he sprang to his full height, his left arm lithely flexing, upward. The ball sped, without sound, a smear hurtling. He pitched another, a slow lob, into the empty curtains as I neared him.

We walked toward the park, over the print of the studs of rugby boots in the hard earth, our two pullovers swinging at our necks. I shared a sodden orange with him. He put the whole of his half into his mouth, and flicked his fingers clean. I could hear his stomach making abrupt noises. Months before, he had told me it was the result of rheumatism of the abdomen. But it was only colic, a wind-pain. My father had told me. He did not excuse himself; he passed the cricket ball, subtly, from one hand to the other.

In the park, he put it in his pocket. We sat on a bench beside the swings where children were shrieking. I could not meet his eyes because of the children who were standing on the swings behind him, in my field of vision. Their movement made me dizzy, a blur of bare throats tilted, a coat-tail flapping, or legs flung wide, their skin the pink of chicken flesh. I stared at the knot of my own hands.

'You make a prayer,' he said, as if he were calling out a list of figures, as if he were chanting, 'you make a prayer out of the dealings of your day, out of all you have done, and all you have undergone; and you offer it up, you see, without words, in silence, to silence. Then you go to bed, feeling no whit better.'

He meshed his hands intensely, drove them against each other till they seemed like grapnel hooks or pliers. I knew from the mesh of his hands.

'I'm going over the top,' he said. 'It's like a gull dropping, slowly, from a vast sky into a vast sea. I'm not deep, you know. I wish I were. Believe me. It has to do with love, you see. You can be hurt; and you can be hurt so well, you start to love. I've only been hurt. And now it's like a gull, dropping.'

Behind him, a bunched child flashed in the high arc of the swing, howling delight and terror.

Cool of the evening air, our arms goosepimpled, yes, and the light plunging like horses into the rhododendrons, we returned by the practice nets. He said:

'A bearfight. That's what we need.'

I had not the heart to refuse him. We locked and tussled, like a drunken dancing team, calling out as if in difficulties; our laughter was too loud. Poised there, fastened to each other, thrusting from each other, he tripped me; I fell, heavily. He pounced upon me. I could feel his heart, pulsing on bone. We lay still. My lungs pained me like heartburn. A woman passed with a Dalmatian dog. She stopped, startled. Then she went away, the clasp of her leash jangling. I could hear the noises of grass, crisp as the shell of insects breaking. He rolled onto the ground, off me. The back of his head touched the verge of the rose-bed. He tore a clod from the bank of earth, and, laughing, hurled it after the woman with the Dalmatian dog. Then he sat, cross-legged, working a filament of orange from between his teeth.

'Got it!' he said. 'At last!'

When he left, his hands were in his pockets, clenched. I could see the outline of their bulk. It was strange, not to watch them as they searched for shapes.

He wrote three postcards to me, before the school year began; the hand was his, a cramped writing that became larger. Often, letters at the foot of the card were four times the size of the date and greeting. I knew why this was so, and I was ashamed of my knowledge. I stored them safely in a pigskin wallet.

The first shows a ship of the line under full canvas on a wild sea. Bent backwards, the sails are stripped and the blown water becomes mild. Straightened, the sails fatten and bag, the blue whitens with spume. There is a wind in the photograph, which my father explained. I read the card: 'I chose this because it reminded me of you know what! Well, here I am – in Rome, of all places! Perhaps you will see it yourself some day! Look up vulnerable in your dictionary, and try to use it with your new words. From *vulnero*, I wound. Love Tom.'

The second he sent from France. It displayed a skater, with plaits and split legs, on a blue background. 'I attended a championship at this ice-rink last night!' it read. 'A girl was leading, and would have won the trophy – a silver skater, six inches high! – but she failed to complete the figure of eight: on the verge of closing it, she slipped! I'm writing this in a gallery, full of old statues. Best wishes, Tom More.'

From Antwerp, a month later: two storks on a rooftop by an aerial, their faces quizzical, aged. That was my favourite. I did not even steam off the stamp. He had written: 'Wish I were going south with them! Weather warm still, but temperatures dropping daily! Overcoats appearing in the streets! Best of British for new school year! Thomas More.'

Once, I dressed the mantelpiece with them, my three cards. In their order of arrival, I propped them between the wooden elephants. But I came back, hours later, to take them down, and put them away.

On the first day back, I heard them talking, the two teachers in the corridor. I passed them closely. A man with veins on his cheeks said:

'Punch or judy? A strange bloody chap.'

'I don't know,' the other replied, pleasantly. 'It's the old story, I suppose: heart over head, head over heels. It's for the best. Thinking men are the bane of the church. The Jesuits should be put to work. In the end, it's the down-to-earth, back-to-barracks sort who gets the job done.'

And I knew then. I went through the basement pantries of the priests' house, up the back staircase, past the small oratory of St John of the Golden Mouth, and across the landing to his bedroom. I had to be careful. I had no business being there. But I reached it, without being seen: the door was ajar; I could see, from the stairs, the edge of the frame of the bed, which was brass. Inside, on the floor, I found a book, Volume M of the *Theological Encyclopaedia*. The words of its contents were stamped on the spine of the cover: Matter, Morality, Mysticism, and a supplement on Mariology. Beside the volume lay a kidney donor card, his book mark. In the corner, his *Victory*, my model, our sign, stood in a polythene drape. The mainmast had been broken, the bowsprit trailed the boards. The desk, the prayer stool, the photograph of the lady with the blue hair-clip, and the lithograph by Munch had all been taken out. The words on the face of the book that was left had changed. They were like things you find in a toolbox – old, cumbrous things.

Outside, under the windows, a master and a pupil were pummelling a door which would not yield.

'Is it locked,' the master said, loudly, 'or is it just stiff? Give it a bit of a heave.'

'I think it's locked, sir,' a boy said.

'Skip round and get the key, like a good man,' said the teacher. I did not hear the boy running for the key, who cannot have been using the concrete path. I knelt beside the radiator below the blinds that clunked and knocked against the sill on which three upright butts supported three soft pillars of ash. Moreover, I said to myself. Nonetheless; furthermore: perhaps.

I said nothing in the classroom. I hunched, my arms rigid,

staring at my lap. But the world came closer. It brushed the tall windows, like high grass tapping slyly, with a noise of fingers, a slow fretting of hands. I wanted to shut it out; still, I overheard myself, listening. The dean of studies came into the class, to take the roll-call. I sensed him in my vicinity. But I was paying too much attention. I did not answer to my name.

FATHERS

'In the lost childhood of Judas, Christ was betrayed.'

I was half-way through my homework when my father put his head round the door.

'There's a good programme starting, old man. About the Nazi death camps and the Eichmann trial. I thought you might be interested.'

The night before, it had been a special report on the fate of the white rhinoceros in Zambia; and on Sunday, a documentary about the shanty towns in Rio. We'd had the television for six months, and my father still played with it like a new toy.

'I have this poem to learn the first three verses of, Bill.'

'I can give you a note,' my father said. 'This programme's important. I want you to see it. Come on down.'

He took his smock off as he went downstairs, wiping clay and crayon from his hands onto the tough cloth. He could never get rid of those stains. Even on holidays in the caravan, away from work, his fingers smelled of the studio.

My mother was doing her nails in the study when we came in. She held her hands in the air like a prisoner to dry them while my father fiddled with the contrast button and the vertical hold.

'I hope it's suitable,' she said. 'I don't want him having bad dreams.'

The voice in the television began to speak up.

'Eichmann is not however a satanist or sadist. His domestic life was both modest and moral. When he was promoted from Untersturmführer to Hauptsturmführer, his first action . . .'

'Here it is,' my father said. 'This is strong stuff, old man, but you have a right to know. The day your mother and I married, ten thousand children were gassed at Auschwitz. I went out that morning to buy flowers.'

He stood at the fire and looked into it, working the dottle from the bowl of his pipe with a pipe-cleaner. Then he came over and sat down beside me.

There was loud music. A map appeared. It was a map of Europe on which shadows were spreading like ink stains to show where the armies advanced. I glanced at my father. He was stroking his beard and nodding his head. I looked above the television, then beneath it; at the knobs; at the screen.

A boy was holding a model train in front of a soldier who struck him with the butt of his rifle so that the boy fell down and lay in the road. The voice was saying dates and places like the names in the Brothers Grimm. Heidelburg, Bucharest, Birkenau. My father put his hand on my knee.

'And you see the people standing round?' he said.

Two soldiers were dragging a man by his collar along the pavement. They passed an old man who took off his hat. Then they let go of the one they were pulling, and they kicked the old man until he kneeled down.

'Bravo. Bravo.'

My photograph was on top of the set beside the Madonna my father had made. I looked at the picture of me in my Communion suit, and at Mary taking her breast out of her blouse to give it to the baby on her lap. I did not want to see the rabbi in the snow with his face burnt.

'Would you look at that?'

'It's not fair,' said my mother's voice. 'He's too young.'

My father waved his pipe at the television. I had not seen him so upset since the programme about the baby seals.

'No man is an isthmus, Mark,' he said. 'No man. On the Last Day, it won't help to conjugate a Latin verb. Did you feed the starving? Did you visit the prisons?'

A woman walked into a yard where soldiers were smoking and lifting box cameras. She started to take off her clothes, wobbling as she pulled her dress over her head. When she opened her stockings, she fell down, and curled up like a baby with her stockings bundled around her feet.

'If not, then to Hell with you. For saying it was none of your business. For saying Pass the salt.'

My father tugged his beard like a bell.

'Are you finished?' my mother said. 'Shall I pass the plate now?'

'Mark understands,' said my father.

He went out in a bit of a huff.

My mother began to fix the cover on the couch, working it down into the edges, straightening the pattern.

'He's not content to be a father. He's not content to be a husband. He's not content to be a sculptor. He has to be a Good Man.'

My father was working with a blowtorch when I went in. He kicked the plug, and turned up his goggles.

'The soldier fought bravely before the city walls,' he said.

I thought.

'Fortiter miles ante urbis muros pugnavit.'

'Father and son went up the mountain quickly to the altar.'

That took longer.

'Pater atque filius in monte celeriter progressi sunt ad altarem.'

'Fair enough,' my father said.

He pulled his goggles down and started the torch. I sat on a box and watched the fantail from the white jet. He shouted at me over the noise.

'What do you think?'

'It's lovely. What is it?'

'It'll keep the wolf from the door,' he shouted.

'And the roof over our heads,' I called.

The Stations for the school chapel were in a pile beside me. Jesus Falls For The Third Time and Jesus Is Comforted By The Women. The parents had complained and said it was their money because Jesus was naked except for the thorns and you could see everything. My father's picture had been in the paper but it was before he had his beard. One parent had come up to me and said he respected my father and would I tell him, and I told him yes.

'Bill,' I shouted.

When he took off his goggles, there was a mark on his forehead.

'Yes, old man?'

'Just Bill,' I said.

I couldn't settle down to sleep, Whenever I closed my eyes, I saw the old rabbi and the corporal who was striking a match to set fire to his beard. Another soldier had given him a bucket of horse manure to put out the flame, but the rabbi would not do it. He kept shaking his head.

I started to look at the stain on the ceiling which was like a map of Italy, and I named the cities, the rivers, the churches. When I closed my eyes again, I smelled sulphur. I didn't breathe. I went deep in the bed. A floorboard creaked.

It was my father. He was lighting a cigarette on the landing outside, listening to hear if I was asleep; standing in the darkness.

*

'In the name of the Father and of the Son and of the Holy Ghost,' Fr Wilson said.

'In the name of the Father and of the Son,' I said. I was looking at the poem we had been told to learn.

Fr Wilson leaned against the blackboard, inspecting his shoes.

'Today promises well for Fr Wilson,' he said. 'Today is a fine April morning, and each member of this class knows his poetry. Isn't that so, Colin my friend?'

'Yes, Father.'

'Would you subscribe to that, Andrew?'

'Yes, Father.'

'Fine. The first three verses, Andrew. The first two verses, Andrew. We were all in bed an hour ago, and it wouldn't do to tax the mind. I know you've made a special effort not to disappoint poor Fr Wilson for the third time running.'

I knew better. Andrew Masterson had been warming his hands on the hot pipes before class, wrapping them round the bars till the tears ran down his good eye.

I was right. He got through seven lines and came to a stop.

The class was silent. I stared at my desk-lid, at the cartoon of the Nazi goosestepping on the cover of my jotter where someone had written: Sieg Heil, The Sculptor's Son.

Fr Wilson parted his lips so they made a sad sound.

'Andrew falls for the third time.'

'I tried, Father.'

'Are you stupid, Andrew?'

'Yes, Father.'

'And lazy, Andrew? A lazybones?'

'Yes, Father.'

'What does that make you, Andrew?'

'A stupid lazybones, Father.'

The class laughed.

'Our Lord died on the Cross for you, Andrew. And you can't learn three verses of a poem for Him.'

Fr Wilson nodded his head up and down in patience, side to side in disbelief. He held up the note for the Dean.

'Goodbye, Andrew.'

'Goodbye, Father,' said Andrew Masterson. He walked up the aisle; and the boys tittered, moving their satchels to let him pass. When he took the slip of paper from Fr Wilson, he got down on his knees. But he was only tying his shoe.

I didn't know that I had stood up until I saw the class turning to look at me, a rush of white faces like underneath leaves when the wind blows them back. There was a shadow coming in front of me. I saw the map, and Bill's face, the rabbi knotting his bootlace, and Andrew curled on the ground with his pants at his ankles. What was an isthmus?

'You're a bully. He can't help not knowing, and you knew he wouldn't get it right. You knew.'

Bill. Bill.

I felt the touch and grasp of hands pulling me down into my desk. Then the hands stopped. I saw mouths opening and moving, Fr Wilson speaking, gesturing to Andrew Masterson, and Andrew sitting down, staring at his book without moving his head; and my nails with biro marks on them: a small hair, an eyelash, on the second nail.

'. . . to have an intercessor, Andrew.'

'Yes, Father.'

When I looked up, the bell had rung, Fr Wilson had left the classroom without his books, and the boys were looking at me, taking their books for the next class out of their satchels.

I waited after school until all the boys had gone. Then I walked to the bicycle shed. I was afraid I would meet Fr

Wilson, and he would be ashamed. I wanted to be home so that I could tell my father everything that had happened from the beginning. He would look at me then the same way he had looked at me the night before when he had pulled down his goggles and I had said: Just Bill.

As I put my bag on the carrier, I heard the noise of twigs. Andrew Masterson came out from behind the hedge. Colin Dennis and Mick the Nose were beside him, each of them trailing a stick in the gravel.

'Hello,' Andrew Masterson said.

'Hello,' I said.

'Hello again,' he said.

'What do you mean?'

'We want to help you with your homework,' he said. 'The three of us want to.'

He flung his leg over the bike and sat on the saddle.

'I love your bike,' he said.

Dennis and Mick the Nose were marking zeros and crosses in the gravel with the sticks.

'I wish my bike was as nice as yours,' he said. He rocked it with his weight so the front wheel strained against the iron prongs in the wall.

'Go easy,' I said.

He stood on the pedals and leaned over.

'I hate to say this but I think I might have warped it.'

He pressed down on the handlebars until the front wheel buckled in the iron bracket and a spoke stuck out.

'Butterfingers,' he said.

He bent down to open the valves on the tyres.

'It'll be easier for you,' he said, 'to wheel it home.'

They were killing a pig in the yard behind the handball court. I could hear its cries peak, like a fast car braking.

I began to cry.

'I forgot what I came for,' he said. 'It was to say thanks.'

I sat down on the gravel and curled in a ball at their feet. When they saw I was ready, they started. But I felt far away. I felt I was behind the hedge, watching.

Their boots rose and fell.

'It's about the rain forests of the Amazon,' my father said. 'And the ozone layer.'

'I have to work, Bill.'

'The serious student, old man. The serious student.'

'You can tell me about it later.'

But he came back a moment later.

'I don't think I'll bother,' he said. 'I'll work for a while. Keep the old wolf from the door.'

He stood, waiting. I looked at the bits of a horse-fly on my wall.

'And the roof over our heads,' I said.

Then he was happy, and bounded down the stairs, taking them two at a time.

I put away my Latin. Below me, I heard a hanger clatter in the wardrobe as my father got his smock out; the rasp of a match on an emery board; and the dull whoosh of the torch as he pressed the foot-switch.

I had to go down.

'What did you do tonight?' he said.

'The subjunctive.'

'No less. Do you know,' he shouted, 'if you keep learning like this, I'll be more of a hindrance than a help soon.'

I watched the flame peel from the jet of the torch and drop in pellets on the floor. Quick droplets of bronze glistened.

'I might have been warned,' I said.

'Monitus fu . . . monitus fuerim. Is that it?'

'I don't know,' I said.

'This is my beloved son in whom I am well pleased,' he shouted.

'You do it, Bill.'

'I've forgotten everything I knew, old man.'

He stopped the torch and slung it in its harness.

'You must be tired,' he said. 'It was hard luck about the puncture. Did you think of locking the bike?'

'It's safe.'

'Trust in God and tie up your camel,' said my father.

I lay in my bed and looked at the stain on the ceiling. I wanted to think about the churches and the squares my father said you could not see for the first time without having to cry. But when I closed my eyes, the woman fell over her stockings and lay on the gravel with her bottom showing; and I stretched out my hand to touch it.

I got up and went across the landing to my parents' bedroom. In the pitch-black, I groped along the chest of drawers until I could crouch at their door, feeling the draught on my ankles. I had to be sure that my father was all right, that he was breathing.

'Cut your nails first, Bill. It hurts.'

Bill's voice: my father's voice.

'O Jesus.'

'Honour us with a verse or two, Andrew,' Fr Wilson said. 'Unless Mark objects. Do you object, Mark?'

'No, Father.'

Masterson fought his way down twelve lines, and collapsed. I had been afraid he might finish. Before class, he had smiled at me as he doodled with a pencil, tracing a coin through tissue paper. But I had kept myself to myself.

'What do you write above your exercises, Andrew?'

'What, Father?'

'The Latin, Andrew, the Latin.'

'Ad Maiorem Dei Gloriam, Father.'

'Indeed. Translate that into modern English for the sake of the uninitiated.'

'To the Greater Glory of God.'

'A bold claim, Andrew.'

Fr Wilson inspected his shoes.

'Homework,' he said, 'is not much to write home about. It's small stuff, by and large. It's not staffing the missions or tending the sick or touring the prisons. But it pleases God that you should do it for Him. To say that you're doing it for Him, and not to do so having said so, is to do what, Andrew?'

'Father.'

'It's to commit the act of a bounder. The act of a cad.'

He held up the note.

When Masterson had left the class to go to the Dean, Fr Wilson called me. I was studying my desk-lid, not looking at anyone.

'The next verse, Mark. I'll keep time on the tin whistle.'

The class was uneasy. Everybody laughed.

'Go on,' said Fr Wilson.

The seat clanged when I stood up. I thought of the woman with the stockings. I wanted to be with her. She would take her breasts out of her blouse and set my head on them; would cover my face with her hair.

> 'Then out spake brave Horatius,
>   The captain of the gate.
> "To every man upon this earth,
>   Death cometh soon or late;
>   And how can man die better

Than facing fearful odds,
For the ashes of his father,
And the temples of his gods."'

From the floor below, I heard the splashing of the strap. For a moment, I was sorry for Andrew Masterson, and sorry that the heating had been turned off that morning so that he had gone to the Dean without burning his hands.

'Fathers,' said Fr Wilson. 'Ashes of his fathers.'

'Fathers,' I said. 'Fathers.'

NEPHRITIS

'It begins with nephritis,' the consultant said, 'and it goes on from there.'

Jonathan could not decide the word he was looking for. Was it *terminal* or *terminus*?

'Is it fatal?' he asked.

'Yes,' the consultant said. 'We call it . . .' but just then the nurse who had shown Jonathan in and given him the *National Geographic* to examine for a half-hour, put her head round the door.

'Doctor,' she said, 'your wife says fine, but where and when, and is it all right if she leaves your off-white shirt out?'

'8.00 at Robbie's,' the consultant said, 'and no, it isn't. The cream one won't go with the club tie. Tell her this is senior faculty. Tell her the whiter-than-white one.'

Jonathan was afraid of asking the consultant a second time what he was dying of.

'So it begins with nephritis and it goes on from there,' he said.

'You got it,' the consultant said.

On the way out, the nurse called Jonathan over.

'Mr Wursmelt,' she said. 'On your Bluecross it says Wursmert; on your Mastercharge it says Wursmelt. What is it?'

'Wursmelt,' Jonathan said.

'Wursmelt is much nicer,' the nurse said.

*

Who could he tell this great thing to? Beth would not want to know. It had been five years since the divorce, and two since they had last slept together. Anyhow, he didn't know where she was now, or who she was with. There was his brother in Boulder, but Chuck would not know what to say, and it was unfair to put a person in a spot. One could not simply lift the phone and say 'Hi, Chuck, I am dying of something that begins with nephritis and goes on from there.' It would be an imposition.

Jonathan stopped at Just Browsing, the bookstore two blocks away from the Angel of Intercession Hospital. There was a coffee-bar at the back near the Science Fiction alcove where everybody brought the sex books to leaf through; and behind that, there was a men's room where he went and sat down in a cubicle with his trousers round his knees for a half-hour, and stared into space and read the graffiti and noticed a telephone number that was almost the same as his own.

People came and went. Jonathan was afraid to come out of the cubicle while someone was in the men's room: they would be sure to notice that he had done nothing. He tried to do something, but nothing happened. So he waited until the last hand-dryer had stopped working. Still, when he did come out into the coffee-bar, he knew that everyone was looking at him very obviously. The bookstore manager kept an eye on him too. Jonathan took a book on astrology from a shelf, and began to read Chapter Five.

'I want a piece of coffee-cake and a coffee too,' he said, avoiding the stare of the bookstore manager.

'The man wants a piece of coffee-cake and a coffee too,' the waitress said, serving him.

Jonathan's eyes watered.

'I am dying of something called nephritis,' he said.

'So?' the waitress said. 'I'm dying of boredom. The manager

is dying to get home. You're dying of whatever. We're all dying. Meantime, you owe me.'

But she came back a moment later.

'You look on the level,' she said. 'You mean it?'

'Would I lie?' Jonathan said.

'Not here,' the waitress said. 'Not in here you're not. I get off at 5.30, I have a date for 6.30, my hair's a mess, and my horoscope says at all costs avoid stress.'

Next morning, Jonathan called his psychiatrist.

'Long time no weepie-weepie, Jon,' Dr Smudgeon trilled. 'You fancy a weepie-weepie?'

'I'm dying,' Jonathan said, 'of something that begins with nephritis and goes on from there.'

'No kidding?' Dr Smudgeon said. 'You get your nephritis round here at 4.15, and we'll straighten it out.'

When Jon arrived at 4.15 Dr Smudgeon was squeezing in a saxophone player with a halitosis problem. He sat in the ante-room, and examined the *National Geographic* he had examined the day before. There was an article on a Zulu enthronement, a piece on a mining industry in Nebraska, and a shorter piece on the courtship ritual of the ant-eater. He whiled away the time, looking at the boobs of the Zulu women, and wondering.

Dr Smudgeon took some convincing. Jon had to tell him the consultant's fee before he believed him. Then he folded his hands; his face fell.

'This pains me, Jon. I am pained by what you tell me.'

Jon's eyes watered.

'There are four stages,' Dr Smudgeon said, 'each clinically observable. First, you're confused. Then you get mad. Then scared. Then mean. Then fat-al-is-tic.'

'That's five,' Jonathan said.

[41]

'What are we talking?' Dr Smudgeon said. 'Numbers? There are four stages, Jon. You are at Stage One. You feel this can't be happening.'

'No,' Jon said. 'I know this is happening. And I feel shy.'

'Jon, Jon,' Dr Smudgeon said. 'Who's the expert?'

When Jon got up to leave, Dr Smudgeon slid a book across the desk.

'For you, Jon,' he said. 'Tolstoy's *The Death of Ivan Ilyich*. It tells the story of a failure, a little man who has done nothing, experienced nothing, loved nothing, cared for nothing. He is told he is going to die. Bedoinng! It might help. It might help you, Jon.'

Jon gave a farewell party for his relatives and friends. Also, he wrote to Beth. 'Dear Beth,' he wrote, 'I am dying of something that begins with nephritis and goes on from there. I am giving a farewell party for my friends and relatives. I know it is five years since the divorce, and two since we last got together, but you are more than welcome. You know that. Your affectionate ex-husband, Jon.'

Beth did not come. Chuck could not make it either. But Jon's boss made it, and his wife and her boyfriend and his boyfriend. Most everyone made it. Jon went out onto the balcony and thanked God that there were so many people he could call on, and to think that he had called them on the Wednesday for the Friday coming. He mentioned this in his speech.

'I feel very humble that you should all make it,' he said. 'There is plenty of food and plenty of booze too. I want to see it all gone. And I should like to say a special word of thanks, of real appreciation, to the caterers. Thank you, one and all, those whom I have known a long time, and those whom I have come to know and to value by meeting them here for the first time tonight.'

Everyone was very nice, going. And the boss's wife, who had always only nodded at Jon so that the celery stalk in her mouth bobbed up and down, pressed his hands as she left, and said 'I think you're just *wonderful*.' Not alone that, but when she came back a minute later to retrieve her doeskin glove that she had mislaid in the bedroom, she had said it again.

Jon lay back on his pillow, smelling a faint trace of eau-de-cologne on the border of the duvet, and decided to remember the whole evening again, from the very first to the very last moment.

The next day, he called Dr Smudgeon.

'I am going to Italy,' he said. 'I am going to die in the Eternal City, or some nice resort where I can hear church-bells.'

'That's nice,' Dr Smudgeon said. 'That's constructive, Jon.'

A half-hour later, the doctor called back.

'Jon,' he said. 'I'm interested in your case. I'm writing up my PhD on Bereavement Structures, and I want to lighten it, leaven it, get a little of the Small Man, the Middlebrow, into it. Jon, send me postcards: how you feel, what you're going through, what angers you.'

'You think that could be useful?' Jon said.

'Jon, I'm talking National Book Awards.'

'I would be honoured,' Jon said, taking more care than usual not to use contractions. 'I would be honoured, Dr Smudgeon.'

When the phone rang the third time, Jon was startled. He had not noticed it was getting dark already.

'Jon,' Dr Smudgeon said. 'My kid collects stamps. Why not? Kids go through a stamp phase, they go through a coin phase. My kid's at the stamp phase. So, on the postcards, Jon, as many *different* stamps as you can manage. For Timmy. Maybe some Vatican stamps if you're in Venice. I joke, Jon, I joke. The psychiatrist is not without a sense of humour. As many stamps as poss., OK?'

'Shall do,' Jon said.

The resort he chose was on the Adriatic. It was called Poggio, but that was all right. Jon would have preferred a more sonorous name, but, in every other respect, Poggio looked just like what a Mediterranean port should look like. There were men with moustaches, women in black with enormous boobs, cafés where sailors stubbed their cigarettes on white metal table-tops, children that peed against the running boards of old motor-cars, fat nuns, thin nuns, tall priests, short priests, fishing nets on the wharf that people stood beside to have their picture taken, and American students with Canadian flags on their backpacks to whom Jon would always reply in the one bit of Italian – or was it Spanish? – that he knew.

'Che sera, sera,' he would say, whenever they approached him.

Mostly he walked the waterfront; sometimes, he sat in bars. Once or twice, while he was sitting down, he had the feeling that he was in an elevator that was descending too quickly. Then he would order a beer, and not finish it. How strange it was to think that, out of all the people in the place, he alone had been singled out to be afflicted (or was it inflicted?) with something that began with nephritis and went on from there.

He met a young French woman, who had known two people at the Sorbonne. Her name was Suzanne. She had wet lips, fingernail polish on her toe-nails, and was a little tubby from a high-dosage oestrogen pill. She was in Poggio to make lire in order to journey on to Athens to make drachmai by minding babies for women who could afford that kind of thing. Then she would travel by train, boat, and foot, to Istanbul. When she got there, everything would work out.

'Perhaps not,' he said. 'You may be seized, and locked into a harem. You may be violated abundantly.'

'Slower, please,' she would say. Finally, she asked him. 'And you, what do you do in Poggio?'

'I die,' he said, 'of a sickness.'

'You what?' she said.

'I go aaaahhh!' he said, clutching his side.

At last, she seemed to understand. After that, they slept together. She would lie her head on his shoulder; all night her mouth wet him. He would play with her as she slept, and walk his fingers up and down her back when the sheet fell off her down the side of the bed.

Jon needed to be certain. He had the desk-clerk translate for him. 'I am dying of something that begins with nephritis and goes on from there,' he said to her. She answered hurriedly. Her distress was very obvious to Jon. His eyes watered.

'She say,' the desk-clerk began, 'that she suffer for you. She say that she will not be-lieve this to be so. She say you are too strong, too handsome, to be sick. She ask: is it contagious?'

A Franciscan monastery had not quite closed at the top of a hill overlooking Poggio. Jon went there, in the funicular. He found a young monk – or was he a priest? – sitting, twirling the rotative postcard stand.

'I am dying of something that begins with nephritis, and goes on from there,' he explained. 'I want to lay my head down in this place, if that is permissible. I would, of course, make a contribution towards whatever.'

'My son,' said the monk, 'level with me. Are you for real?'

'Would I lie?' Jonathan said.

'I believe you,' the monk said. 'I believe you. The important thing is not to be morbid. The Christian stands for affirmation. Christianity is about struggle, about immersion in a world in which the proletariat of the industrial West and the living dead of the Third World are ground down beneath the feet of the consumer capitalist. Do you realize how many people in this world would *eat* Purina Cat Food? And you talk to me about nephritis.'

'It's not nephritis,' Jon said. 'It begins with nephritis.'

'It has to begin somewhere,' said the monk. 'You have to let it grow. You have to make it an experience of growth. Only then can it be a growth in experience. You want to stay, you got a bed. Any questions?'

'Yes,' Jon said, 'St Francis . . .'

'Probably gay,' said the monk. 'Rome has the files.'

'What I mean,' Jon said, 'is this: did St Francis say Brother Death or did he say Sister Death?'

'He was very flexible,' the monk said. 'He was a very understanding man.'

When Jon returned to the hotel, the assistant manager was waiting in the foyer with the desk-clerk.

'Mr Wursmelt,' the assistant manager said. 'I'm so sorry, so very sorry. Nephritis, they tell me. Still, you must understand: this is a family hotel. If anything – God grant otherwise – were to happen; if, in short, you were to become acutely nephritic, other guests might think it was the food. My competitors would make hay of your most lamentable illness.'

'It's not nephritis,' Jon said. 'It only begins with nephritis.'

'But where does it end, Mr Wursmelt? Is that not the question? Where does it end?'

Later that evening, after the beef stroganoff, after the apple-strudel, after the cappuccino with peppermint schnapps, after the blue pill and the green pill and the vermilion pill, Jon sat in his chair in the dining-room of the hotel, and felt the elevator feeling. When it passed, he went to reception and settled his account.

'You will come again to Poggio,' said the girl at reception.

'I am going aaaahhh!' he said, clutching his side.

'I understand,' the girl at reception said. 'You are right. It is very beautiful.'

When he went to his room, Jon called the hotel operator.

'I want to make a collect call, long-distance,' he said. 'To a Dr Smudgeon in Manhattan.'

'Give me the number, sir,' she said. 'I ring you back.'

Minutes passed. In the background, the radio clock blinked.

'Dr Smudgeon says he can't take collect calls, Mr Wursmelt. He says that it's very important that you should understand his reasons. They are strictly financial.'

'Of course,' Jon said. 'I'll pay.'

'Shall I put it on your bill, sir?' she said. 'Your account says Worsmelt, but I notice that your Mastercharge says Wursmelt. What is it?'

'It begins with nephritis,' Jon said, 'and then it gets so much worse.'

DANIEL'S DIALYSIS

When Daniel finally decided to come off dialysis, he rang his sister Harriet.

'Harriet,' he said. 'I have finally decided to come off dialysis. I am tired of being in pain, I am tired of having to go to the hospital twice each day for no good reason. More than anything else, I am tired of being sore at night when everyone's phone is on the answer machine.'

'You listen to me,' Harriet said. 'This is a very important decision to reach so suddenly. You must give yourself time. You must go through the whole decision-making process more carefully, and not just call me because your day's gone phut.'

'Harriet, I have taken three days over this thing. I have gone at it from every angle. I have sat so long in the bath thinking it through that my fingertips look like raisins.'

'What can I say?' Harriet said. 'If you'd called me earlier to tell me that you were going to call again to tell me that you were going off dialysis, then I might have been able to organize something appropriate to say to you. But you give me no notice. Here I am, slicing up liver into slices of liver, my hands all yukky from it, and you call me to say that you are going off dialysis. What can I say?'

'I don't want you to feel that you have to say anything, Harriet. I love you. You are my only surviving sister.'

'I am the only sister you ever had,' she said.

'Well, of course, that is true figuratively. Literally, however, we should not all together forget Celia.'

'Celia!' Harriet said. 'Cot deaths don't count, Daniel.'

'Harriet,' Daniel said, 'wishing no disrespect to poor Celia, could we get back onto my dialysis for just a moment?'

'Daniel Horngrad,' Harriet said, 'you just stop saying that horrible word to me. You are really, really trying to depress me. I want you to call me tomorrow, and I want to hear you say: "Harriet, it is early morning here on the other side of the block. Outside my window, I can see the eucalyptus tree. I can even smell it. Look, there's a woodpecker! How lovely they are, woodpecking away. Look, I can see a plane too, high up! How wonderful that people can do that. Fly, I mean. Harriet, forget my talk about coming off of the dialysis. I was just depressed. I am back on my pills now, and I know how good life is. I will stay on the dialysis."'

Next morning, Daniel called Harriet.

'Harriet,' he said, 'it is early morning here on my side of the block. Outside, there is the eucalyptus. Every year, it gets bigger. Some years, it seems to get bigger than other years.'

'Can you smell it?'

'Sort of. I have the extractor fan on.'

'Is there a woodpecker?'

'There is a woodpecker, but he is not woodpecking. He is just sitting there looking thoughtful.'

'Are you back on your pills?'

'I was never off them.'

'Say it for me,' Harriet said. 'Say the rest for me.'

'Harriet, I want to come off dialysis,' said Daniel. 'Today, I am so sore that I want to cry, but I am a grown man. Also, I hate the drive to the hospital. I hate the nurse who talks to me as if I was a child or dumb. Why should I have to put up with that, when I am seventy-one and will be seventy-two next year? I am old enough to be her father, if I was poor, and her husband, if I was rich. Also, I am afraid. I wake up sometimes, and put on all the houselights. Last week, the neighbours called when they saw the lights going on all over the house, even the barbecue patio and the pool. They thought I had been broken into.'

'Turn off your extractor fan, Daniel,' Harriet said. 'What's this about a barbecue?'

'I cannot play golf any more,' Daniel said. 'I cannot carry my groceries. Sex is out of the question. They have taken the Benny Hill Show off of Channel Two. That was the one thing, the one thing, Harriet. They have put on some corny old rubbish.'

'Haven't you got a Sports channel?'

'I have lost interest in everything except the things I cannot have,' Daniel said to Harriet.

Who could argue with that? It was just like Daniel to get a lot of weird notions into his head. He was so stubborn, Harriet thought. The word *obdurate* had been written for Daniel. If you looked up the Directory, you would find it there. 'Obdurate: a word that describes Daniel Horngrad perfectly. Obdurate as Horngrad: a folk expression in Mountain View, California.' What did he mean about coming off dialysis? The doctors had told him he would die if he did that. Was he deaf? He was just like his father. He was just like his uncle too. It must have run in the Horngrads.

'Daniel,' she said, when he finally answered the phone on the twenty-sixth, if not the twenty-seventh, burr. 'Daniel, why didn't you answer me? Do you realize how irritating it is for a person to listen to those burrs? Where were you, Daniel?'

'I just didn't care to answer. I hoped you would stop ringing and just hang up.'

'Daniel, I may be sixty-seven, but I miss very little. You are beginning to behave very strangely. Are you taking the right pills?'

'I am taking a bourbon,' Daniel said, 'and I am looking through the catalogue that the mortician sent me.'

'What mortician? What are you talking about? Are you ga-ga, Daniel? Are you forgetting to put your socks on under your shoes? Are you not going to the bathroom when you should go to the bathroom? Are you your father's son, Daniel?'

Daniel was not prepared to get into that kind of conversation.

'I have chosen something very simple,' he said. 'Something plain and unpretentious. I am going to have an upright headstone, with only a small amount of fretwork. The lettering will be incised, and the mortician's people will come out each six months for ten years to clean it, and make it brand new all over. What it says is . . .'

'Daniel, I am not deceived. You *are* beginning to behave in a very cuckoo manner. Is this a Horngrad legacy, I ask myself, or is it you, Daniel?'

'What it says,' he told her, 'is this: Daniel Horngrad was born in 1910. He died in 1982, at the age of seventy-one. That will be on the top, but there will be plenty of space for you, Harriet, if you should decide against going down to San Diego when you are seventy.'

'You are unwell, Daniel. You need the ministration of professional hands.'

'People might stop,' Daniel said. 'People like to get their figures right. They get very angry if their figures don't work out. They are going to think that I should have been seventy-two when I died, and not seventy-one. That way, it would make sense. I can see them stopping to sort it out in their heads; stopping right at the spot where I am buried. My memory will be preserved.'

'Daniel,' Harriet said. 'I am going to put the phone down right away, and I am going to call a priest. He will be round to you before you can put on your socks.'

But Daniel put the receiver on the work-top, and wandered off to dunk another ice-cube in his bourbon. He liked the way it hissed. Then he flicked through the channels he had until he hit the ads on Channel Four. There might be an ad for Playtex, or the new perfume where the girl bends way over in her leotard, and then the camera zooms in, and then the shot goes soft-focus, and the English voice reads the credit-line.

'Daniel,' Harriet's voice said from the work-top in the dinette. 'Daniel, will you please put the telephone back? You are so unwell, Daniel. Do you know that?'

The priest meant well, but he was very young. First he tried taking Daniel's side against Harriet.

'She is something,' he said. 'She is something else.'

'She is menopausal,' Daniel said.

They were standing on the barbecue patio. The priest did not know what to do with his bourbon. It was terribly strong, and the ice was taking forever to melt. Besides, merely holding it incapacitated his right hand, which he would much rather have used expressively, in conjunction with his left hand, the way he had been taught at the diocesan Body Language work-outs. Would it be obvious to bend down and place it on the cement patio for a few moments?

'Gee,' he said. 'I thought she looked a little older than that.

I thought she looked like sixty-five. But very elegant. A very elegant sixty-five.'

'You never get over it,' Daniel said.

'What?' said the priest. He made as if to put the drink down on the ground, but stopped midway.

'The menopause,' Daniel said. 'Are you all right?'

'Me? I'm fine, just fine. I'm admiring the cement'

'The cement?'

'Cement seems very prosaic,' the priest said. 'But can you imagine the twentieth century without cement? Can you imagine New York without cement? When people talk about the twentieth century, they talk Hitler, they talk Stalin, they talk Mao, they talk Picasso. Whoever talks cement?'

'You should put that in an essay,' Daniel said. 'You could call it "The Forgotten Factor".'

The priest had finally put his glass down. Both his hands shot into action.

'How could anyone ever get tired of just looking?' he said, moving his hands like a Frenchman.

'I understand what you are saying,' Daniel said. He was feeling dizzy. Was it the hands, or the bourbon, or the other thing? If it were dark, he would put on all the house lights.

'I mean, look at that eucalyptus,' said the priest. 'What a thing to have in one's back garden. It's so ... majestic. I mean, you don't have to be religious to feel how awesome a eucalyptus tree is.'

'The kids used come from next door to play in it,' Daniel said. 'They had a tree-house. Then they got older. Now they call me Mr Horngrad.'

But the young priest had found his stride.

'Have you ever gone to that magnolia bush, and looked into a magnolia? I mean, it's incredible. It should be in the

Chicago Art Institute. I could spend months just looking into a magnolia.'

'And Johnny calls me "Sir",' Daniel said. 'I cleaned his bottom when he was two years old. He calls me "Sir". When he passes in the car, he pretends to be adjusting the mirror, or there's something falling out of the glove compartment. He ducks.'

The priest decided he would give it a last shot.

'Have you ever looked into a magnolia?' he demanded.

'Not for months,' Daniel said.

'I was speaking metaphorically, when I said "for months",' the priest said. 'Why do you want to ridicule me? Why do you want to antagonize me?'

Daniel felt ill. He reached out and switched on the pool lights. The water glinted a little, and became more green. Two eucalyptus pods bobbed at the deep end.

'I'm not,' he said. 'You misunderstand me. Why did that silly woman disturb your afternoon? I have nothing to say to you.'

'You are something else,' the priest said. 'You are really something else.'

The party was Harriet's idea.

'People are going to talk,' she said. 'You can't stop them talking. So my own point of view would be: give them something really substantial to talk about. I want to be able to hold my head up about this whole thing. I don't want to just have people sniggering.'

'What more can I do?' he said.

'You can throw a party,' she said. 'It would be sophisticated; it would be kind of European. You might say a few words. Your friends could say a few words. I'm talking thirty people, cocktails, semi-formal. Soft music, our music.'

'And then?'

'Then you go upstairs to bed. In the morning, we take you to the funeral parlour. You could be wearing your party clothes, or that nice suit you bought for the Insurance dinner.'

'The clothes are secondary,' Daniel said. 'I want to be buried with my clubs, and a ball in each hand.'

'Have it your way,' she said. 'Just so you look spruce for the party. If it goes well, people will see that you have been through the decision-making process in a very mature manner. If it doesn't, then I inherit a fool brother who couldn't meet his payments, and had to stop the treatment. Daniel, I couldn't bear having people be nice to me in the Co-op.'

'We'll have a party,' Daniel decided.

It would be quite an affair. Harriet had the college kid who was rooming in her house come over to set up party lights round the barbecue patio and the swimming pool. After that, he trailed some wires under the carpets and out the French doors onto the cement strip where the sunbeds were stacked.

'Speakers,' he told Daniel, who was sitting down on the diving-board, a bourbon in his hand, watching him.

'Speakers?'

'It's a great effect,' the boy said, 'to have music coming at you from the magnolias. And the sound-waves make the pool-water vibrate. Very romantic.'

'That would be groovy,' Daniel said.

The boy tried to be nice about it.

'We don't say that anymore,' he said. 'We say awesome. Or nice.'

'I say nice too,' Daniel said. 'It's an OK word.'

The boy was beginning to regret the assignment. This was not worth twelve dollars.

'It's all right,' Daniel said, getting up. 'I have to go to the hospital. For the last time. Then I don't have to go again.'

'That's nice,' the boy said. 'That must make you very happy.'

Harriet had said eight for eight-thirty. Everybody arrived punctually. The drive was crowded. People parked on the grass. One man reversed into the rose-bed.

'I knew you wouldn't mind, Dan,' he said. 'I knew you had bigger things on your mind.'

'You should talk to Harriet,' he said. 'Everything goes to Harriet.'

But there was Jan! And Linda – was that really Linda? – right behind him. Paul McDonald too, looking terrible. The McDonald genes, Daniel thought. You can't beat the genes.

'Linda, you look lovelier than any woman with a grown family should.'

'Paul, how well you look, how fit and fresh you . . .'

The guests – and Harriet, damn it, had known just who to call – were quiet. It was not every day that you got invited to this kind of affair. People stood straight, folded their arms, nodded gravely. No one seemed quite sure what it was that Daniel was dying of.

'Cancer. Didn't you know?' said Linda to the Goodmans.

'How terrible,' both the Goodmans said. 'How terrible for Daniel, and for Harriet too.'

'He only told his closest friends,' Linda said.

'Where is the cancer located?' said Mr Goodman, who had been pre-medical through four years of Business School.

'Where is it *not* located, would be a better question,' Linda said.

At the other end of the room, the cancer had been flushed out of hiding.

'Imagine,' said Paul McDonald. 'The worst of all: both lungs.'

The smokers were very discreet, bending toward the fireplace to blow their smoke into it.

Harriet thought that things were going marvellously.

'People are a little inhibited,' she admitted. 'But what can you expect? You *are* dying, Daniel. You may even be the first dying person they have met. You can't blame them if they forget that, underneath it all, you're still the very same person, the same Daniel.'

Daniel had been touched by the occasion. As people arrived, they had all taken his hand, holding it tightly and for a long time, looking into his face. 'Daniel,' each of them had said. 'Daniel.' And everybody had brought something. It was like a fraternity potluck; it was like the old days.

'I have brought you your favourite cheese, Daniel,' Linda had said. 'I have brought you Camembert.'

'I have brought you a copy of that Charlie Kunz track you have been talking about for forty two years, since you heard it for the first time at the Munich Beer Festival,' Denise Goodman said.

'I have brought you the costliest Bordeaux that I could lay my hands on at such short notice, Daniel,' said Jan. 'You were always a terror for a good Bordeaux.'

Small wonder that Daniel was, if not actually overcome, well on the way to feeling quite emotional.

'Small wonder, indeed,' said Harriet, to whom he confided this information. 'You are surrounded by friends who care about you. How often does one have an experience of community? How often does one enter into relationship? We are such intermittent creatures, are we not?'

'I feel good about this, Harriet,' Daniel said. 'I feel warm inside.'

*

Harriet made that remark the keystone of her speech. After she had talked for a few minutes, she invited those present to volunteer to do likewise. A little reminiscence would not be inopportune. Rather would it be appropriate.

Jan spoke first.

'I remember,' he said, 'that game of tennis we had, Daniel.'

'We had many, Jan,' Daniel said warmly.

'Ah! But there was one, Dan, there was one in particular. I lost it. You won. As we left the court, the sun was sinking. It was one of those moments. You put your arm around me as we walked off the court. You put your hand on my shoulder. I stopped. "Jan," you said. Just that. Just once. "Jan." It's the little moments, isn't it, Dan?'

'It's the little moments, Jan.'

'Jan is always telling me that story,' the blonde said. 'It means so much to him.'

'I remember,' Denise Goodman said, 'the Christmas tree we put up, Daniel.'

'We put up many,' Daniel agreed.

'No,' Denise said. 'Just the one. It was that time Harry was away in Vancouver, and you came over, and it was snowing. Imagine that. Snow. Anyhow, you got the tree up out of the store-room, and we sat there together putting all the wire bits together, and so forth. We had a fire, and President Eisenhower was speaking.'

'As if it were yesterday,' Daniel said, staring into his bourbon.

'I remember you throwing the silver stuff onto the tree, after we got the bells on, and so forth. I remember thinking how elegant you were, like you were waving to someone, and all the silver stuff just folding round the branches. The whole tree shimmered.'

'Denise will never forget that tree, Daniel,' Harry

Goodman said. 'Myself, I remember the fishing holiday we had, me and you, up in Tahoe. In the log cabin, among the trees. That first time, we got nothing. N-o-th-i-n-g. I was very demoralized. You turned to me, and you said: "There'll be another time, Harry. There's a trout down there that's going to make a mouthwatering smell up at the log cabin." I remember thinking: Damn, I just wish I had Danny's way of seeing things. I just wish I had that kind of deep patience.'

'Harry never gets tired of that story,' Denise said.

Daniel was afraid that his eyes were beginning to fill up.

'Excuse me a minute,' he said, and made for the library. As he left the room, everybody burst into spontaneous applause. Daniel heard it stop after a time; then he could make out talking again. He stood in the darkness in the library, listening to the voices.

'Am I breaking something up?'

It was the blonde who had come with Jan. She was holding her wine glass very precisely with two fingers by the stem. Perhaps she was tiddly. Where were her shoes? She had seemed so much taller, and blonder, with her shoes on.

'The garden is like a ship,' she said, moving away from Daniel to the window.

'Everything is like everything else,' Daniel said.

'Because of the party lights,' said the blonde. 'They light up the pool-water, and make it so greeny. It's just like the deck of a ship.'

'The sea is very black at night,' Daniel said.

'But the pool-water on the ship's deck is greeny,' said the blonde. 'Can you hear it?'

'The pool?'

'The sea. Going ssmmusshh, ssmmusshh, very softly, ever so softly, along the sides of the ship.'

'You are a beautiful person,' Daniel said. 'You have a beautiful mind.'

'Listen harder. Awwk, awwk! That's a gull. Brroomm, brroomm! That's the funnel.'

'Are you intelligent as well as sensitive?' Daniel said to her.

'Not very.'

'What are you into?' Daniel asked.

'I am into the Tarot pack. I am into the British Royal Family. I am into labradors. I am into losing weight.'

'I am into losing sleep,' Daniel told her.

'Do you want to look at me?' the blonde said. 'Would it make you feel any better?'

'You are so sensitive,' Daniel said.

So the blonde unzipped her skirt, and stepped out of it, and stood in front of Daniel in her pink blouse and little Maidenform briefs. She put out her arms like a skater, and turned and turned in front of him, but slowly.

'You are very blessed,' Daniel said. 'You have a beautiful figure.'

'Would you like to touch me?' she said.

Daniel thought about this.

'No, thank you,' he said. 'I think it would spoil things.'

'Iiiccckkk!' she said dreamily, as she turned with her arms out. 'That's the wood on the deck creaking.'

In the next room, they had started to sing his song, not too loudly.

When everyone had gone, Daniel was left alone with Harriet.

'You have another six to seven hours, Daniel,' she said. 'Then you will fall asleep. Then you go into a coma. When I stop by tomorrow, it will all be over. Have you organized your suit?'

'Everything is laid out,' Daniel said.

'Where will I find you?,' she said, bashing one of the embroidered sofa cushions into shape. 'Will you be in the bath, like a Roman? Or will you be in the bedroom?'

'Harriet. I am doing a sort of re-think on this decision,' Daniel said. 'I am going through the whole decision-making process from A to Z one more time.'

'What are you talking about, Daniel?'

'I never realized that I had friends like I have,' Daniel said. 'Everybody was so much nicer than I ever remember them. They were so concerned, so feeling. Why I went into the library was because I got emotional about it.'

'Daniel, you are behaving strangely again. What you are saying is not consistent. It is very weird.'

'I was thinking that tomorrow I might call you, and say: "Harriet, the sun is coming up, and all the aluminium in the kitchen is shining with it. I cannot smell the eucalyptus because I have wrecked my olfactory system by smoking, but other people can. The woodpeckers are going to have their woodchip quota by ten at the latest. They are going at it, hammer and tongs. Me, I am going to the hospital."'

'Daniel Horngrad, are you determined to make a complete fool of yourself? Are you determined to expose me, the only sister you ever had, to the ridicule of my contemporaries? How do you think Denise and Jan are going to feel when they find out that you tricked them, that you manipulated them, that you let them down? What are people going to say? What is the *Mountain View Herald* going to say? How can I shop in the Co-op, if you go ahead with the dialysis? Have you any insight into the selfishness behind everything you are just after saying?'

Daniel could say nothing. Where was the bourbon? Why had he not touched her legs at least? What would have been wrong with touching her legs?

'Daniel, are you listening to me? I want you to go straight to your room, and take an anti-depressant.'

'I am out of anti-depressants,' he said.

'You can have mine,' she said. 'You can have two of mine. I just want to see you behaving normally again.'

When Harriet left, Daniel walked around the house, turning on the lights. First the bedroom, then the bathroom, then the studio, then the library. Finally, he switched on the pool lights and the party lights. The pool-water gleamed. Mosquitoes darted over the surface. The magnolias were very quiet.

'Ssmmusshh,' Daniel said. 'Ssmmusshh.'

He could smell the eucalyptus.

THE STORY OF THE GERMAN
PARACHUTIST WHO LANDED
FORTY-TWO YEARS LATE

THIS IS what happened.

The Bowmeester family was sitting down to a late supper. Strictly speaking, this statement is inaccurate: two of the Bowmeesters had, in fact, already sat down; Mr Bowmeester (hereinafter to be called Bowmeester Senior) was folding his Tuesday copy of the *Norwich Chronicle*; and Mrs Bowmeester was having a lot of bad luck with her quick-mix chocolate cake, in the kitchen. But you will have to grant that the inaccuracy is minor; and, insofar as everybody – both Bowmeester parents, the boy Bowmeester, his sister who is called Moninne – is engaged *in the process* of sitting down to supper, the grammatical inclusiveness of the opening sentence may stand.

The main thing is, you get the picture. And you certainly get the name. If you have not got the name by now, you should skip this story, and go on to the one in the library, which is about sudden death, or the one before this, which is about slow death. If you cannot manage Bowmeester, you are not going to be able to cope with Dietrich Fosskinder, who is the person alluded to, periphrastically, in the title of this story.

One last time: a family (of Dutch extraction, but that is not important); supper; a cake that has not worked out; a provincial newspaper. Implications: the family is patriarchal: Mr

Bowmeester is reading a paper; it is his wife who has to experience the failed cake-mix. Implication: the kids are hungry. Implication: this is a short story with teeth.

I will have to give you some more details, but only four, since we are already running behind schedule. There is an African beaver coat on the arm-rest of the sofa, which Moninne bought at a swap-shop; it is an all-right coat. There is an oval wedding photograph on the mantelpiece, which is probably the Bowmeester parents' one, or perhaps their parents'. The glass door of the clock on the mantel is a little dirty with flour smudges: whoever has been winding it, has also been working with flour. There is a yellow stain on the edge of the sofa cover nearest the castor: tea or urine. If the first, it can be removed. If the second, it is most likely a dog – a dachshund? – but there is no smell of a dog in the place, and, besides, Bowmeester Junior abreacts to dog-hair. Now a human being is hardly likely to have done it. We are dealing, let me tell you, with a very normal family.

'How's the cake coming?'

'The cake's not coming.'

'The cake's not coming?'

'The cake's not coming.'

'Oh well, if the cake's not coming, the cake's not coming.'

Bear with me: I am just trying to establish verisimilitude.

Moninne was still drying her nails. She handled her cutlery with precision. Bowmeester Junior was trying to flick something from his nail onto the carpet, but it kept sticking to his thumb. When he tried to flick it off his thumb, it stuck to his finger. Bowmeester Senior was taking the news about the cake badly.

'Quick mix,' he said, rather elaborately.

'Have you ever tried baking?' Moninne demanded.

'Look who's asking,' Bowmeester Senior said.

'What's this about?' Bowmeester Junior said. He had finally got the thing off his hand onto the carpet.

'Cakes.'

'Is it coming?' Bowmeester Junior said.

That was when they heard the noise. Noise is perhaps too strong a word; sound, on the other hand, is too weak. Everybody heard it. It had come from the apple-trees at the bottom of the garden. The Bowmeester family listened hard. The night had become very quiet. Not a stick cracked underfoot; not a leaf gave up (and why should it? It was, after all, early spring); not a breath of wind disturbed the weather-beaten branches of the Bowmeesters' apple-trees. Things were as still as a mouse.

'Mice are not quiet,' Moninne said.

All right. Things were as quiet as the grave.

'Who knows if the grave is quiet?' Moninne said.

Point.

'I shall go out to whatever has made the noise,' Bowmeester Senior said. He did up the top button of his shirt, and began to knot his tie.

'Don't you set a foot outside this house,' Mrs Bowmeester said. 'Who knows what it is? What you want to go bringing Things into the house? Dirt on your shoes. Nasty dirt over my carpet.'

'Someone might have thrown a bottle over the wall behind the apple-trees,' Bowmeester Junior said.

'It might be a meteor, or a bit off a satellite,' Moninne said.

'Or an owl doing unforeseen and objectionable things to a rabbit,' Bowmeester Senior said.

'It might be someone going to the toilet,' Mrs Bowmeester said.

'It will not go away,' Moninne said.

'It will go away,' Bowmeester Senior said.

[71]

'Make it go away,' his wife said, running her hand through her hair, and making it all floury.

Mr Bowmeester opened the door. Outside, it was very dark. Strictly speaking, this was not out of the ordinary. After all, it was eight o'clock, and the clocks had not yet gone forward. In two weeks, they would; but not yet.

'It is at times like this,' Mr Bowmeester said, 'that one realizes the true value of hearth and home. Of domestic plenitude. Of what one has to be thankful for.'

They would always remember him like that, the other three decided. Pensive and handsome, standing there, going out to whatever might have made the noise.

'We'll wait for you,' they cried, which was, strictly speaking, unnecessary, since the room was not too large.

When he had gone, Mrs Bowmeester looked at the clock.

'It has stopped,' she said to her remaining family. 'Your father has gone.'

Bowmeester Junior examined the hands of the clock.

'It stopped twenty minutes ago,' he said. 'Just before the story started. It is all jammed up with flour.'

Mr Bowmeester walked through the darkness. Here and there, he knocked against roots. Once, his foot walloped off the haft of a rake. In the dark, he could smell apple-blossom and dampness. It had been drizzling. His suede shoes would be ruined. Wasn't there a step there somewhere? He put his foot out cautiously, as if he were testing the water.

High up, a cloud moved over the bit of moon that had been there. Three stars came out. That made twelve. When he was nervous, Mr Bowmeester counted the stars. Where he could, he gave them names. Where he could not, it was another part of the Milky Way. That got over the problem.

Now his heart was beating loudly. Still, the doctor had said that exercise was all right. Sex was equivalent to running five miles, there and back. On the other hand, you could die of shock. He had often heard people saying 'He went and died of shock.' If it was not true, they would not say it.

'Who are you?' he said to the darkness.

It had nothing to say to him.

'Where are you?' he said to the darkness.

But the darkness was not about to tell him.

Mr Bowmeester decided to go back. He turned slowly. If he went very quietly, nothing would pounce. He could feel the darkness stroking his neck. In front of him, there dangled a pair of boots.

Mr Bowmeester kneeled down. He could hear his heart as if it were coming out of speakers. His head got warm and heavy. The boots went up to legs. The legs joined the rest of a body. There was a face. At least, there was a mask and goggles. Overhead, silk and nylon drapes glistened like polythene among the upper branches of the trees. And above that, all the stars had gone in.

'Are you Jesus?' he said. 'Have you come to haunt me?'

'Jesus does not haunt,' said the mask. 'That is the job of the Holy Spirit.'

'Are you the Holy Spirit?' Mr Bowmeester said. It was a fair question.

'I am a German pilot,' said the face behind the goggles. 'My plane was shot down. I baled out. Help me to get down from this tree. The wind is piercing. My mind is dismayed by images of conflict. The stars have been put out overhead.'

'Are you stuck up there?' Mr Bowmeester said.

'No,' said the German pilot. 'I landed on open ground, but I had so little to do that I arranged myself up here, the better to appreciate the view of the surrounding countryside under starlight.'

'You have not lost your sense of humour,' Bowmeester said, 'and your command of English is most impressive.'

'Where would one be without a sense of humour?' said the German pilot. 'One would be totally in the dark. My English is not bad. A trifle bookish, perhaps. But I do not command it. It commands me.'

'Where did you learn to speak as you do?'

'Anything can happen in a short story,' the pilot said. 'My author thought it would be as well if I spoke excellent English. Besides, it was not to be expected that you would be able to converse in fluent German. You can see that he has made allowance for almost every contingency.'

'What happens next?'

'For the moment, this moment must suffice. You must stand beside me at the foot of the apple-tree, and meditate the strangeness of this happening. I must remain here, waiting for assistance, my being slumped in obscurity.'

Bowmeester had recovered himself. Now he was all efficiency.

'Let me help you,' he said. 'I can loosen the straps of the parachute. Are you wounded?'

'I am thirsty,' said the German pilot.

'Would you like an apple?' Mr Bowmeester said kindly. 'It is eighty per cent water.'

'That would be nice, but I would much rather an apple-juice.'

A suspicion had begun to form in Mr Bowmeester's mind. Then it started to emerge. But this should not surprise you: formation and emergence are the characteristic habits of a suspicion.

'We are not at war,' he said. 'We are at peace. How can you say your plane was shot down? We were at war with

Argentina quite recently, but that is all forgotten. Are you an imposter? Are you a lunatic? Are you a practical joker? Are you a Soviet interloper? Are you something that has welled up out of my imagination? Where are your papers?'

'My name is Dietrich Fosskinder,' said the pilot. 'I was shot down over Norfolk. I have been falling ever since. Moments ago, I woke up, and I smelled apple-blossom and dampness. Then I heard a noise, the sound of a man stumbling. I thought it might be an animal. I was afraid it would be a Dobermann Pinscher. Then you spoke to me. I knew that my author was not striving for verisimilitude, but I was confident that he would not go so far as to confer human speech-patterns on canines.'

'We are in safe hands,' Mr Bowmeester said. 'We will not be manhandled.'

He had unfastened the last of the parachute straps. The German pilot fell the few feet to earth. His ankle twisted fluently beneath him.

'Would I have said "fluently"?' said Mr Bowmeester. 'There is somebody at work here, beside ourselves. I can feel a benevolent presence.'

'I can feel pain in my Achilles' heel,' said the pilot. 'I am bleeding internally.'

Mr Bowmeester put his head under the German pilot's armpit, and hoisted up his trunk. Then he helped him limp among the apple-trees towards the house. It was still there. He had been a little afraid that it might go up in smoke. Stranger things had happened at night. It might just go up in a puff of smoke.

'Not unless the people in the house play with fire,' the pilot said.

'I was speaking figuratively,' Bowmeester Senior said. 'I

meant it might be annihilated, dissolved, done away with. I meant it might be pulled up into the sky on wire-strings, like a stage-set.'

'We would call that a *Himmelfahrt*.'

'I would call it the end,' Mr Bowmeester said.

There was great confusion in the house when the pilot was introduced. Mrs Bowmeester wiped her hands on her kitchen-apron, and got off most of the flour. Then she shook hands.

'I have inside staff,' she explained to the pilot, who was very dashing. 'It's their day off.'

Moninne had rushed off next door to smell herself under her arms. She was all right. All she need do was sprinkle a little toilet-water around the collar of her blouse, and behind her ears. She always had her period at the wrong time, she thought. Always. She always felt bottomy at the wrong time.

'How are you?' she said sweetly.

Bowmeester Junior nodded.

'Just drop in?' he said.

First they ate. Then they cleared away. Then they washed. Certain things were not in themselves crucial, but they helped to preserve a sense of the natural order of things. They were more important than ever when you found a German pilot dangling from an apple-tree at the bottom of the garden.

'All I saw was these two feet,' said Mr Bowmeester.

He had told the whole story. They were enthralled, even the pilot.

'Did you think I was dead?' he asked.

'Not after I checked your blood pressure,' said Mr Bow-meester.

Moninne could not help herself.

'Were you not so afraid?' she said to the pilot.

'I have never been anything else,' he said. 'One gets used to it.'

'When was the worst moment is what Moninne means,' said her mother.

'After I baled out. Falling through the darkness. Around me, stars wheeled; the planets spun; my chute flowered above me like a jellyfish. Cold burned my fingers, my eyes stung in the rushing blackness. Hoar hung heavy on my cheekbones. Ice inched upwards on my two greaved calves. Sleep overcame me. Jaded, my jaw dropped on my breastbone. Dozed I did, for all hours. Waking, I wondered. My balls were frozen.'

'You poor man,' Moninne murmured.

I did not. I said it quite audibly.

All right. All right.

'Why must men suffer so?' she said, and it sounded better coming from her.

'But what were you doing up there?' said Bowmeester Junior.

'I was escorting Heinkels to bomb Norfolk,' the pilot said.

'What a mean thing to do,' Bowmeester Junior said.

'It *was* somewhat anti-social,' Bowmeester Senior said.

'But you were only obeying orders,' said Moninne, who had finally opened her third button. It took hours to de-freeze a fridge. She knew that, but surely people were different.

'What else are orders for?' said the German pilot.

He was feeling comfortable now, his feet wedged among the fire-irons in the fireplace, and his back leaning against the fattest of the bean-bags. His wine had been sitting at the fire for a half-hour, and it was still ice-cold. Anything can happen in a story; and anything had. Besides, they were nice people, even if slow on the uptake.

But the most important question had not yet been asked.

'Why did it take you forty years to land?' Bowmeester Junior wanted to know.

'Were you that high up when you baled out?' Moninne said.

'It did not seem like forty years,' the pilot admitted. 'It was more like the wink of an eye. Yet the falling seemed never to end. Far above me, the dead stars glittered. Their light was so tired. They had long since folded up. Their light passed by me. Some of it struck on my shoulders and sleeves. Some of it spotted my hair.'

It was true. It was like paint.

'There are things you cannot ever brush off lightly,' the pilot said.

'How will you cope?' Moninne said. 'The world is so changed. We have colour photography, sun-lamps, satellites, detergents that kill every germ you can name, Italian and Mexican cuisine, synthetic contraceptives. Most of all, we are at peace. We are not at war.'

'This is Problem Number One,' Mr Bowmeester said. 'You must get used to the thought of peace. You must adapt to the thought of travel. I have been to Germany. I have been to the red-light district in Hamburg, though I did not exactly go in. I have been to Checkpoint Charlie. There is a picture to prove it. I have been to Krefeld, on business.'

'Krefeld I know,' the parachutist said. 'Krefeld is a nice place.'

'Krefeld is OK,' said Mr Bowmeester. 'I am not crazy about it.'

'I have travelled too,' said Moninne. 'To Greece and to Southern Italy. I have never been in Mallorca. I could not even point to it on a map.'

She was rather proud of that.

'Problem Number Two is a problem as well,' said Mr

Bowmeester. 'You must see that you do not fit in. You must
see that you do not quite belong.'

'I will go native,' said the German parachutist, looking at
Moninne.

'But not completely,' she said. 'You must always be different. You must always be the man who has fallen for forty
years. You must never forget your position. People are forever
doing that nowadays. All we are left with is the Royal Family,
and even they make speeches.'

'Tomorrow morning, I will bury my parachute. Better still,
I will burn it.' The wine had gone to the pilot's head. How
good it was to be warm, to be among people, to smell women,
to come into a room and know that there were women in the
area. The young one opposite, with the unpronounceable
name, had a particularly strong spell.

Smell, you mean.

Smell. She had taken off her boots and placed them beside
the poker. She wore tights, with a ladder in the left leg. Left
to look at; right to wear. He had been falling for so many
years. Now he could begin to climb again. He would like to
start by climbing that ladder.

'You mustn't think of burning it,' Mr Bowmeester said. 'It
would be useful for so many projects. I could use it to insulate
the rabbit hutches. I could use it to lag the immersion. The
Imperial War Museum might want it for their collection. Who
knows? Perhaps they have no such thing in their files.
Besides, it will bring back memories for Mrs Bowmeester.
She used to fold them for the boys.'

'Did I?'

'Of course you did. They used you on a poster, you had
such a cheerful way of going about it. Nothing made you
happier than folding parachutes.'

'What did you do, Dad?' Moninne wanted to know.

'Me, I filled sandbags. Thousands of them.'

'When I first joined the Luftwaffe,' the German pilot said, 'it was the proudest day of my life. My father embraced me; my mother put up her face to be kissed. They were not by nature overly demonstrative. You can imagine my embarrassment, my gratification. Then I walked arm-in-arm with my sister around the restaurant area of Dresden. Her behaviour towards me was quite improper; I suspect that she was trying to disguise the fact that we were siblings.'

'You must be very striking in your uniform,' Moninne breathed. 'In my copy of *The Illustrated History of Lingerie* there are photographs of male models in fine Gestapo uniforms, reclining in *dix-huitième* chaise-longues while scantily attired women pull languidly at their boots. One cannot be sure what may or may not occur thereafter. But I doubt that such women would be in a position to go home again.'

'Moninne, you are talking very funny,' said her mother.

Mr Bowmeester felt that enough was enough.

'Enough is enough,' he said. 'There'll be time to talk again tomorrow. Our guest, our honoured guest, must be tired.'

'I am fresh in fact,' said the German pilot. 'I have not been getting up to very much for about forty years.'

Mr Bowmeester insisted. He felt that this paragraph was running beyond itself. One had to bear in mind the bladder capacity of the average reader.

'There is a time for beginning paragraphs, and there is a time for ending them,' Mr Bowmeester said.

They rigged up a camp-bed beside the fire for the German pilot. Moninne brought him a bolster and an eiderdown bedspread; Mrs Bowmeester rummaged about until she found ointment for his chilblains. Bowmeester Junior had walked down the garden to where the slick, translucent folds of the parachute drowsed on the branches of the apple-trees. The moon frosted its tauter parts.

'Until I touch this, I am not going to be deceived,' Bowmeester Junior said.

It was not like sail-canvas at all. It was like the feel of women's things as you walked through the undergarment department toward the boys' department. And it was wet.

He ran back toward the house, wiping his fingers madly against his trousers.

Moninne stole in to the pilot round midnight. She took the rubber-band out of her hair, and let it down.

'It suits you down,' the pilot said.

'Are you not sleeping?' Moninne said.

'I am asleep,' he told her. 'I am having a dream. Also, I am being dreamed. In the process, I wake up, and I find a young woman with an unpronounceable name and a strong body-odour kneeling by my camp-bed, letting down her strawberry blonde hair.'

'I am going to wash your feet with my hair,' Moninne said.

'That would be rash,' the German pilot said. 'You would go away again with the smell of feet in your hair.'

'But perhaps some of the light would rub off on me.'

'It has long since dried in,' he said apologetically.

'You must make the difference for me anyhow,' she said. 'I demand that you make the difference in my life.'

'I am too afraid,' the German pilot said. 'I am afraid I will be dreamed in a way I do not want. I am afraid I will be dreamed back on to the apple-tree. I am horribly afraid I may find myself falling again. I want a normal life. I want high-jinks, kids, a choice of vegetable with my dinner, all the Sunday papers.'

'How can you do this? Is that what you fell all those years for?'

Her voice was starting to wobble.

'Stop, please,' he said. 'Tell me what you can smell.'

'Nothing,' she said.

'Smell harder.'

'Myself,' she said. 'The cake that did not work out. You. The socks drying on the clothes horse beside the fire. Blood in my mouth where I bit my lip to stop crying.'

'Up there, there was nothing to smell. For forty years.'

He groped for her. But she drew back.

The Bowmeester parents were pillow-talking.

'You see my point,' Mrs Bowmeester said. 'I don't deny he is very charming. But this is not a novel. In a novel, one has more time. Anything might happen. He might even settle down, and make a match with Moninne. But in a short story, rush is undesirable. I can't simply drop round to this or that person tomorrow morning, and say to them: "Guess what? We have a house-guest. He dropped in late last night. A fly by night. A ship passing. Come and meet him. He is not going to go away. He is not a tourist. He is a pilot."'

'I see your point,' Mr Bowmeester said.

'Besides, we have been misled by the author. When he said that something would happen, and asked us if he could choose our household as a representative family, we were given to understand that something appropriate would occur. Not that the sky would fall in on us. The surprise I can accept. Surprise keeps you young. It's the *inconvenience* I resent.'

'Not to mention the damage to the apple-trees,' Mr Bowmeester said.

'Absolutely.'

'Why couldn't he have fallen on the road?' said Mr Bowmeester nastily.

'He never thought,' she said. 'Sheer thoughtlessness.'

'Just like a German,' Bowmeester Senior said. 'Just like Jerry.'

'Besides, I never imagined a pilot,' said his wife. 'I thought a Pools man perhaps; or a solicitor with news of some cousin in New Zealand.'

'Solicitors are all the same,' Mr Bowmeester said. 'Take. Take. Take.' He was still thinking about his apple-trees.

'Or a boyfriend for Moninne,' said his wife. 'I mean a real boyfriend. A nice boy.'

'He'll have to go,' Mr Bowmeester decided. 'There's no place for him here. Did you see the way he just walked in?'

'I knew something bad would happen tonight,' his wife said. 'My cakes always turn out.'

'Typical bloody Hun,' said Mr Bowmeester. 'Just walked in, out of the blue.'

'What this whole episode lacks,' Mrs Bowmeester said, 'is, to use the most right word that I can think of, a sense of *decorum.*'

'You took the word out of my mouth,' her husband said.

They told him at breakfast. But they were nice about it, and perhaps a little afraid. Germans were very violent people. So they waited until he had finished his eggs, and was on his second cup of tea. Then they struck.

'This is a bit of a volte-face,' he said.

'I never wanted to hear language like that in my house,' Mrs Bowmeester shuddered.

The German pilot was distraught.

'I could make myself useful,' he said. 'I would be an asset.'

'You are a liability,' Mr Bowmeester said. He was rather pleased that he knew some legal language. 'You are a definite liability.'

'I can see the way you've been looking at my daughter,' Mrs Bowmeester said. 'At the part between her throat and her tummy. I've been watching you.'

'I was hoping to have relations with her,' the pilot explained. 'I would find sex with her very fulfilling.'

'How dare you talk like that in front of her parents,' said both her parents.

'I was expecting the paragraph any page now,' the pilot said. 'I was going to submit a draft to the author, for consideration.'

'What did it say?' Moninne said excitedly.

'"His hands found her, wet and waiting. She thrust against him. 'Jesus,' she cried. 'Jesus.'"'

'I would never use the Holy Name in that manner,' Moninne demurred.

The last three words are hard to say together.

Rightio.

'I would never say "Jesus",' Moninne said. 'Who do you think I am?'

'Have you a better one?' said the pilot.

'"Again, his hands reached for her. She drew away, frowning. 'Not now', she said, 'not yet, not here.'"'

'Better let the author decide,' said the pilot.

This is what I decided.

For a long while, he was content to lick her armpit.

'I love your little tuft,' he said.

'You've been there long enough,' she said. 'Go somewhere else now.'

'Enough is enough,' Mr Bowmeester said. 'This paragraph is going nowhere. The point is, you are not wanted here.

Leave us alone. Barge into somebody else's apple-trees. Make a mess of someone else's cake.'

'You cannot just throw me out,' the pilot said. 'Like I was old water, or a broken zip.'

'You are a nuisance. You are a domestic incident. You are a shadow thrown over the happiness of our lives together.'

'But I cannot leave without my parachute,' the pilot said. 'I am nothing without it.'

'If you do not leave at once,' Mr Bowmeester said, 'I shall summon the police. I shall call the Rodent Exterminator. I shall call the Drains Inspector. I shall even call a Doctor.'

'I'm going,' the pilot said. 'But you are condemning me to a fate worse than falling. You are condemning me to the existence of a margin. I shall be a crumpled piece of paper: foolscap crushed into a ball for children to kick.'

'That,' said Mr Bowmeester, 'is your look-out.'

'But you must see my point of view.'

'And what would happen then? Were I to do so, what would be left to me? I would find myself considering the point of view of the veal I consume, of the anthracite I burn, of the apples I gather. Life would become impossible.'

'My parachute,' the pilot said. 'My parachute.'

'You must think us simple folk,' Mr Bowmeester said. 'How can I be sure that you won't drop in on us again? Through the greenhouse panes, or the very roof-tree. What guarantee can you give us? And when did the word of a Kraut mean anything? I have buried your parachute.'

'This I cannot believe,' said the pilot. Panic was spreading through his syntax.

'I have you foxed,' Mr Bowmeester said. 'I have you banjaxed. I went out and did it while you were eating your first egg, just before the paragraph started.'

'You were too busy looking at bits and pieces of my daughter,' Mrs Bowmeester said.

'I appeal to the author,' the pilot cried.

Leave me out of it. I am only ghosting this.

'I appeal to the . . .'

Yes?

'I appeal to . . .'

So?

'I appeal . . .'

Get on with it, for Heaven's sake.

'I.'

The Bowmeester family was sitting down to a late lunch. Mr Bowmeester was folding his Wednesday copy of the *Norwich Chronicle*. Mrs Bowmeester was having better luck with her sponge gateau. Moninne had stopped bleeding, almost. And Bowmeester Junior had been grinning away.

'Look at this lot,' he said.

He opened the holdall, and tipped out the contents. Some of them sparkled and glittered, the way contents should; others did neither.

'German money,' Mr Bowmeester said.

'Hitler marks,' his son corrected him.

'Are they worth anything?' Moninne said.

'You would have to ask a philatelist,' her brother said. 'But I should jolly well think they are.'

'Bully for you,' Mr Bowmeester said. 'What else?'

'A comb. A signet ring. A pencil sharpener. Eye-drops. A rubber-band.'

'That's mine,' Moninne said. 'The rotter. He went and stole it.'

'When did this happen then?' said Bowmeester Senior.

'Last night,' Bowmeester Junior said. 'I went through his pockets. I thought he might have had an Iron Cross.'

'Him have an Iron Cross?' his father jeered. 'They only gave them to men.'

Mrs Bowmeester appeared with an immaculate sponge gateau. They all cheered.

'My cakes always turn out,' she said.

Mr Bowmeester held up his hand for silence.

'Last night, we heard – or thought we heard – a noise. A sound. A disturbance. Something, we thought – or thought we thought – had happened. Perhaps. It was dark at the time. Sound travels at night.'

'I went down the garden,' Bowmeester Junior said. 'I don't like to say this in front of the women. Somebody had gone to the toilet.'

'Big ways or small ways?' said his mother.

'Both.'

'Imagine that,' said Mrs Bowmeester.

'Did you get rid of it?' Mr Bowmeester said.

'I buried it.'

'I went down the garden too,' said Moninne. 'I found bits of a rabbit.'

'Imagine that,' said her mother.

'Did you get rid of it?' Mr Bowmeester said.

'I buried it.'

'And I,' said Mrs Bowmeester, 'I went down the garden too. I found pieces of glass.'

'Imagine that,' said Moninne.

'I got them up with a rag, and dumped them in the bin,' her mother said.

'It is very strange,' Mr Bowmeester said. 'When I went down the garden . . .'

'Yes?' they all said.

'I noticed nothing out of the ordinary.'

Mrs Bowmeester blew dry flour off the hands of the clock.

Then she started winding them round anti-clockwise with her finger.

'What time is it?' she said, happily.

This was more like it.

THE STRANGEST FEELING
IN BERNARD'S BATHROOM

BERNARD WAS almost sixty, and still happy. He liked to bring this up in conversation. It was his only vanity. ·

'I don't expect much,' he said. 'That way, I'm never disappointed. Other people want the sun, moon and stars. When they don't get them, they become bitter. Honestly, there is so much bitterness in the world. If only people were happy with what they have. That's what I always say.'

All his friends in the staff canteen would nod when he said this.

'You're a philosopher, Bernard,' they used to say. 'You're a wise old bird.'

Jack Barrett, his oldest friend, who managed the Curtain Material Section, would chip in here.

'If there's one thing better than an old head on young shoulders, it's a young head on old shoulders,' he said, wiping bits of pastry from the corners of his mouth.

And Bernard would come in on that cue.

'The young people want their houses curtained and carpeted before they move in. They want everything at once, just like that. It was different in our day.'

'A damn sight different.'

Then Carmel Timoney, who worked in the Stationery Department, would bring the whole thing to a close. She would punch out her cigarette at the edge of her saucer, and speak for them all.

'No wonder you look so young, Bernard,' she always said. 'The right attitude is worth a hundred trips to the doctor.'

'Or to the psychiatrist,' Bernard would say, but only if the girl from the Information Desk was sitting at another table, because one had to remember, all said and done, that her brother had been in and out of homes ever since the accident on the motor-bike. If she was sitting with them, he would say something else.

'Or to the priest,' he would say.

'God forgive you, Bernard Brennan,' Carmel would say in mock horror. 'Wait until I tell your wife.'

That was the pattern of Bernard's life. When you thought about it, there was a lot to be said in its favour. It was all very well to talk about action and adventure, but the truth was you had enough to contend with from day to day. Bernard's life was full of days. It took him all his time just to get through them. Sometimes he thought they would never end. Still, he was good humoured about that too.

'Time probably does fly,' he used to say, 'but you have to wait a long time to get clearance for take-off.'

They loved that.

'You're a laugh a minute,' Jack would say to him.

But his wife had heard it too many times.

'Would you ever think of another one?' she said.

So the next time the topic came up for discussion, he changed it slightly.

'Time probably does fly,' he said to Janet while she was folding shirts in the kitchen. 'But it flies on one engine.'

Secretly he preferred it the other way.

Bernard's day began with an erection, and ended with anti-flatulent lozenges. He hated taking them, even the lemon-flavoured ones, because he had to get out of bed to wash his teeth again. If he didn't take them, the inevitable happened. Then Janet would turn over angrily, taking most of the eiderdown with her.

'It's not fair,' she would say. 'It's just not fair.'

His erection she never noticed. Once he had pretended to be asleep, and rolled over to her side. But she never said a word, then or later. Anyhow, that was years ago. There was no point in wondering about it now. Instead, Bernard wondered about other things. Rainbows, for example. They had to do with reflections and the spectrum, but most people never bothered to find out. They just darted home between showers, or gave out about the weather forecast. But they never once stopped to think: how extraordinary rainbows are. In fact, there was no end to what you could wonder about. Teachers nowadays understood that. When he was at school, you never heard about nature trips. And what about the way in which Religion was taught? You didn't just parrot off any old rubbish anymore. You talked about things, you were open to discussion. Of course, certain questions could never be answered. Take a sixty-year-old dead person. Would that person be raised up as a baby, a boy, a man, or an old man? Not even the priests with beards could tell you that. Or take the way people were different. Why was one person a millionaire, and another man with a spastic child? As to sex, you could wonder about that until the cows come home.

Bernard spat out the hydrogen peroxide he had been gargling. Then he rinsed his mouth with warm water.

'You're a great man for questions,' he said to his image in the mirror.

A face that was almost sixty, and still happy, looked back at him. Its lips were white with toothpaste.

*

That was where things stood, the day Bernard walked into the bathroom without realizing Janet was in the bath. He was the kind of man who likes to shave twice a day. Besides, doing it the old-fashioned way with cream and a naked razor gave one a few minutes by oneself after a day spent behind the counter without any real opportunity for privacy. It made you fresh and alert as well. Most of all, it was a good discipline. Bernard had always known when the rot sets into a man: if a chap stopped shaving, he stopped making the effort. He might as well pack it in. His cards were numbered.

It was a good thing Janet had turned on the warm-air heater over the towel rail. Otherwise she might have heard Bernard opening the door. As it happened, she was sitting with her back to him, fiddling with the taps. All her hair was up under the shower cap that had the design of the little Black and White Minstrel men running round musical chords on it. She was bent forward so that her spine stood out. Bernard could see the red mark of her brassiere strap and, just above the water, the thin print that her panty hose had left across the small of her back. It was ten years since he had last seen her like this. Perhaps it was more.

'Janet,' he said, and was amazed that he had.

But she never heard him. The taps were going full blast, and the steam was rising in clouds. She started punching the water between her legs, and then whisking it, to make more foam. Bernard could see the slippery corner of her breast, and the white puncture-marks of the vaccination weal on her shoulder. Her body seemed very tired somehow. He felt terribly sorry for it, and for her too. In fact, he had never quite experienced such an odd feeling before; he was at a loss what to call it. He had always been very fond of her, of course, but one assumed that. When they had been married at first, there was the other too as well, for a while at least; and then there was the Christmas feeling, good-will and so forth, from time to time. But that was par for the course. That was run-of-the-mill stuff.

Janet screwed the taps shut with both hands. Now he could hear again the high humming of the warm-air heater, its dry gusts reaching him across the length of the bathroom. He was afraid she might sense him then, or feel a draught, or lose the soap and turn around, groping for it in the bath. She wouldn't understand, she would think he was some kind of Peeping Tom, she would have no idea of the sadness he felt as he saw her sitting there, looking ridiculous and forgotten-about and delicate. He felt if he touched her she would come out in a rash around the mark of his finger. If she fell getting out of the bath, her skin would be bruised. If her ankle knocked against the spigot of the tap, the tissue would blacken. Anything might happen. Without her clothes, she was so terribly naked.

Bernard shut the door quietly behind him, and stood for a while in the passageway. Suddenly everything had gone quiet. He couldn't hear the warm-air heater now. His own body-sounds made the only noises: his heart and stomach juices, his lungs taking in air.

'Janet,' he called.

The heater was probably too loud. Or perhaps she had water in her ears. Or maybe she was washing her hair. Would she wash it sitting in the bath or standing beside it, bending over? You could be married twenty-eight years, and not know these things.

'Janet,' he shouted.

Finally she heard him.

'I'm in the bath,' she called out. 'I can't hear you.'

Bernard was determined to make more of an effort that evening. It was never too late. If there was one thing people agreed about, it was that. Of course, it would be silly to talk in terms of a resolution. That kind of talk got you nowhere. It would be better to think in terms of giving up cigarettes. When you stopped smoking, you did so quietly. You told no-one. You just hoped for the best. If you made it through Monday, the chances were you would last through Tuesday too. But there was no use worrying, or looking back. The main thing was to stick at it. That would be his approach. Anyway, if he was suddenly to become attentive, she would probably suspect him. It might even alarm her.

After supper, he began to stack the dishes.

'What's got into you?' said Janet.

'I thought you might be tired,' he said.

'Thanks very much.' But her tone of voice took the good out of it. 'I've been tired for twenty-five years. Watch where you let that gravy drip.'

Still, she seemed pleased. From the way she swung her sandal by the toe-strap he could tell she was chuffed. That was one thing he knew about her.

'You're in good time for your programme,' he said.

'It's on late,' said Janet. 'That's why I had my bath early. There's some football match on, with a satellite link-up. My programme isn't on until ten.'

She cocked her head to one side, and shook it a few times. For a moment, she became strange to him again. He was slopping the dinner plates into the pedal bin, but he stopped to look at her.

'Water,' she said, wagging her finger in her ear.

What was the point? After twenty-eight years, you could hardly walk up to your wife, and say to her 'I saw you in the bath this evening, and I was shy, but not for the reason you might think. It was because you seemed so small really, so helpless almost. I wanted to put my arm around you, although it was not a sexual feeling. It was more a feeling of sadness.'

'You're only making work,' she said to him. 'You're making a mess.'

She was picking peas and a potato-skin off the floor. He let her take the plate from his hand. Then he peeled off the kitchen-gloves. Perhaps it was already too late. Perhaps it would do more harm than good.

Janet examined him closely.

'You're in strange form tonight,' she said. 'You didn't even shave when you came in.'

When she was fast asleep, Bernard put his bedside lamp down on the floor, and turned it on. Then he could look at her without fear of waking her. Something of what he had felt in the bathroom revived in him, but it was not as strong or sudden or strange. In fact, he had to work at it a bit. Face-cream glistened on her cheeks and forehead; her lips were tightly shut. After a while, he experienced a kind of affection, a sort of peace; yet it all seemed willed. What had happened in the bathroom was unselfconscious, and he was wistful about it now. But perhaps it would happen again. Perhaps it would happen more and more often, at the most unlikely times, in the most unexpected places.

Bernard pressed another anti-flatulent out of its foil sheet. He let it dissolve slowly on his tongue. Then he made his way to the bathroom. He could still see the prints of Janet's feet where she had stood under the heater to dry her shoulders and hair, tapping clouds of talcum powder onto her legs so that the white and lemon dust settled around her on the dark carpet. After he had washed his teeth, he sat down on the toilet, and looked at the prints. They were like the marks you see in snow: bird-marks or hoof-marks. There were animals in Asia that had never been seen, Bernard thought. They were known only by the prints of their paws. He had forgotten how small Janet's feet were. They were almost petite. Yet she was not a small woman. She came up to his shoulder.

When Bernard got back into bed, his hands were so cold that he couldn't touch himself with them. He held them away from him until the heat of the bed made them warm again. He knew it would be an hour, perhaps an hour and a half, before he slept. But he was used to that too.

Bernard's third-best suit had a blurred look at the collars and cuffs, and a glazed look at the seat and elbows. In the morning, he put it on, and went to work.

'Have a good day,' he said to Janet.

'I don't know how you get away with that suit,' Janet said. 'Jack Barrett is always dressed like a lord.'

He could see that she knew he was behaving differently. It made her uncertain.

'Don't just stand there,' Janet said.

He could say it now. He had twenty minutes to spare. Janet was still in her dressing-gown too. It was strange how defenceless people seemed in their night clothes. Their work-clothes made them hard again: when they were dressed, they would fight you tooth and nail. But they were clumsy and bashful in their pyjamas, smelling of toast and sleep. He could see why the secret police made dawn-raids. It would be a good thing if the United Nations were to meet in dressing-gowns. Then there would be fewer wars.

'Will you not just stand there?' Janet said. She gathered up the collar of her dressing-gown, and covered her throat with it.

He would say it that evening. Friday night was a good time for speaking out.

'Goodbye so,' he said.

A young black in a brightly coloured shirt sat opposite Bernard on the bus. If you look at them, Bernard thought, they imagine you're being critical; if you look away, they suppose you're being contemptuous. He wished he had bought a newspaper on the way to the bus-stop. It might be a time before he could offer his seat to an old lady. The bus was only half-full, and old ladies made a habit of getting up later in the morning. It would be foolish to stand for a young woman. After all, he was almost sixty. Besides, if they wanted to wear trousers, they could go the whole hog, and stand in buses as well.

Bernard stared out the window, lifting his hat from time to time as the bus passed a church. He had never been very consistent in this practice. At times, he liked to raise it at any and every church, whatever the colour of its money; at other times, he would tip it intermittently, once in five perhaps, or once in six. Today, he touched his hat-brim whenever he saw a church; and he was a little surprised, as he had been before, at how many of them there were, on the way into work.

What had happened in the bathroom was not sexual; and if it was, it was also more than that. Seeing a pretty girl sauntering along the street, and wanting, let's call a spade a spade, to reach out and pat her behind, was one thing; but to walk into your own bathroom, to see your wife sitting in the bath, and to feel sad and shy about it, was another. Not that Bernard was a stranger to emotion. He had his feelings, even if he didn't parade them. Only a week before, he had gone out of his way to minimize the fuss when a young woman was caught with a pair of lisle stockings in the Religious Objects Department. Jack Barrett, for all his palaver, would have prosecuted; but Bernard had talked to her nicely, and said it was obviously an oversight, and would she go back to the hosiery section, and pay for the article there. In the end, she made a bee-line for the side-exit.

Bernard looked down at the black hands in the lap opposite him. Why were the hands of black people, and brown people for that matter, so beautiful? Their fingers were long and tapering; they were like pianists' fingers. It was no wonder the blacks had invented jazz. Now if it was Jack Barrett on the bus, he would not have noticed the delicate black hands. He would have saved up some comment about squashed lips and noses. He would not have been open to the beauty that you can see in blacks, if you take the trouble to look. But that was the whole trouble with Jack. He was a very nice oaf, it was true; first and foremost, though, he was an oaf.

Bernard stood up. He had reached his stop.

'I beg your pardon, sir,' he said to the black.

The man was confused. His legs were not in the way. Still, he drew them in, and watched the nice old chap with a kind of happy face stepping down off the bus.

When the lunch-hour was almost over, Bernard decided that he would, after all, tell Jack what had happened. Carmel had turned away, and was chatting ten to the dozen to the girl whose brother had had the nervous breakdown.

'I walked into the bathroom last night,' he said to Jack, 'and I saw Janet just sitting in the bath. I . . .'

'Carmel,' Jack called. 'Come and hear about Bernard and Janet in the loo.'

'Bernard Brennan,' said Carmel. 'Now at last we know how you manage to stay looking the way you do. I'll have to keep an eye on you, I will.'

'But it wasn't that at all,' Bernard explained to Jack. 'It was the strangest feeling.'

'I think I know the feeling,' said Jack, winking elaborately at Carmel. 'I had a touch of it myself this morning when I went the short way through Trousers, and what did I see?'

'Tell us then,' Carmel said.

'A young lady who was nameless and shall remain so, stretched out on the floor of one of the cubicles, with her feet out like so, as if she was having a baby.'

Jack pushed back in his chair and swung his legs high. There were whoops of laughter. Bernard gave up, and joined in.

'What was she doing then?' he said.

Jack puffed and panted his answer.

'She was holding her breath, and sucking in her tummy, to get the bloody designer jeans on. But her arse wouldn't go in.'

Carmel covered her face, and howled with glee.

'Yes,' said Jack in his normal voice, 'I know about strange feelings. You're a clever old bird, Bernard. A wise old owl.'

Bernard looked at the clock on the canteen wall.

'Time flies,' he said.

'Are we ready for take-off?' Jack said, twisting round to squint at the hands.

'No,' said Bernard. 'We're just coming in to land.'

On the way home he had an inspiration.

A priest would listen. In a sense, and without any disrespect intended, that was what they were paid for. It was downright stupid to have even tried talking to someone like Jack Barrett. What could you expect of a man who put brown in his hair, and wore a gold chain around his wrist? Jack had an answer for everything: it was the easy way out. But a priest would understand. At the same time, of course, it would be unreasonable to suppose that a priest would have had any very similar experiences. That was what the whole argument about celibacy was concerned with. On the other hand, they were men who read, and travelled. They knew a lot, and they meant well, even if they did go on a bit about the joy of service, and the joy of faith, and whatever. It was easy known they had never sold a pair of shoes across a counter.

Finally, Bernard got off the bus one stop short. The Church of the Incarnation was only a stone's throw. Anyhow, he would just nip in, and see what happened; if he changed his mind, he could walk home through the park. But he hesitated at the church railing, and was even more unsure in the church porch, where two small boys were playing conkers with a young curate. His fingers stung when he dipped them in the font: holy water had a way of being cold.

Am I behaving oddly? Bernard wondered.

Inside, there was an old woman leafing through a parish newsletter, and a file of six or seven persons waiting for Confession. Bernard sat down at the end of the bench, and shifted farther up it whenever the queue shortened. He used the muscles of his bottom to do this. It was strange how it brought back his childhood, when his legs didn't reach to the kneelers, and he had to shuffle along the seat on his bare thighs, with the waxed wood cold against his skin. That was what Bernard hated most about churches: they always brought you back to your childhood, as if things were not already difficult enough.

And what was he going to say to the priest? That he was a man of feeling? That would be some kind of start, but it might well seem unusual, the more so if the man hearing Confessions was one of the old school, all gate and no garden. In a way, it was odd to be coming to confess at all. It wasn't even a matter of slip-ups or stabs of conscience: it was more the desire to confess the strangest feeling, and one that, in spite of its own bizarreness, Bernard rather hoped to have again, and even again, if that were possible. Because he had no other feeling to measure it against. True, he remembered seeing the blind children coming out of the home the nuns ran, and being emotional about that, especially when they filed across the road at the zebra crossing, each holding onto the one in front, with an albino at the top of the line. Still, he hardly ever thought about that now. Besides, you would want to be a monster not to be upset about blind children. A middle-aged woman sitting in a bath with a shower cap on her head, and no Brigitte Bardot, be it said, was a different thing entirely.

He was almost the first in the queue. This priest was a quick one. Other persons had filled the bench behind Bernard: a policeman in uniform, which was quite extraordinary when you thought about it, a quite young girl with cold sores on her mouth, and a father and son, the son looking rather fed-up, if the truth be told.

Bernard was next. This was ridiculous. He couldn't walk into a Confession box, and rattle off a story about surprising his wife in the bath. The priest would think he was mad. He might even ask the policeman to throw Bernard out. Worse, he might decide to keep Bernard for ages. He might be one of those very young priests who should have been psychiatrists, and would like nothing better than to open the prisons or sell off St Peter's and all its treasures. If he was, and he found out about Bernard not seeing Janet in the buff for however many years, he would probably go on and on, and end up by wanting to see them together. In the meantime, you would have all those people outside, just wondering why on earth this particular confession was taking so long.

The other people in the queue were a bit surprised when the old man who was next, and had a nice, happy kind of face, stood up and walked off. He must have something pretty weighty on his mind; or perhaps he was a crank; or maybe he had left his gloves somewhere, and just remembered where.

Everybody moved down one along the bench.

When Bernard arrived home, and walked upstairs, he found that Janet was in the bath. At least, she was in the bathroom. He listened at the door, but he could hear nothing. The warm-air heater was on.

'Can I come in?' he shouted.

'What?' Her voice was not terribly pleasant. Of course, she hated shouting.

'May I come in?' Bernard said.

'I can't hear you,' she cried. She was certainly exasperated.

'Please may I come in?' Bernard shouted for all he was worth.

'I'm in the bath,' she screamed.

So he went downstairs again, and hung up his coat, and straightened his tie, and ran a hand through his hair. There were plums in the bowl on the sideboard in the living room, but perhaps they were meant for later. Instead he took a Turkish Delight out of the second layer in the box of chocolates. There were some left in the top layer, mostly nougat, but he didn't care. He would go down to the second, even if she criticized him for doing so. After all, who had bought them?

Bernard sat down, and thought about his day. Perhaps it had been impetuous of him to leave the church. Perhaps he would mention the whole thing from start to finish to Carmel Timoney. He had talked to her about other things, personal matters, in the past, and she had always been helpful. When you thought about it, she was a most obliging woman. Why had he not spoken to her instead of to Jack? But perhaps Jack meant well beneath it all. You never could tell.

Bernard went down to the second layer again, and took out a hazelnut this time. He could hear Janet letting out the bathwater.

Perhaps he had misunderstood himself the night before. Perhaps he had been startled by Janet's plainness and fat. Perhaps he had been a bit appalled that she couldn't make more of herself. No one was asking her to be Greta Garbo, but she might make the effort. Or perhaps he had been tired, or depressed. He had a perfect right to be, sometimes. Maybe it was just as well she hadn't let him into the bathroom with her.

Where was the orange one?

Bernard leaned back, and chewed the chocolate on his good side.

Perhaps it was just as well.

THINGS THAT HAPPEN

OUR EYES are opened in so many different ways.

Frank and Sheila were together in the kitchen. Frank was sitting at the butcher-block table, sifting through the double-glaze catalogue the Rapid Aluminium people had finally sent out. He was not quite semi-conscious yet, but he had high hopes. On the other hand, he was semi-inclined to catch a back episode of 'The Fugitive' on the other channel. The trouble was, that would involve some fine tuning and a lot of fiddling with the hold buttons. Since Monday the set had been snowing. The man had still not come. What did they do all day? Still, it might have been an atmospheric problem. There had been thunder and lightning for three nights now. One time there was thunder without lightning; another time there was lightning without thunder. Either way, the picture had been kaput.

Sheila was still cleaning and polishing at the basin. It would never occur to him, she thought. Not once would it cross his mind to pick up a dishcloth. God knows, she was making enough noise on the work-top: dish after dish, plate after plate, the whole canteen of cutlery, and the silver still to do after all that. What she needed was an au pair. What she needed was a husband who would get up off his backside once in a blue moon.

Sheila pulled open the utensil drawer with a vengeance.

Everything needed to be done: the egg-whisk had egg on it, the pastry-cutter had cake-mix on it and the Japanese knives were so dull you would never think she cleaned them every second week and had them sharpened twice a year into the bargain. Was there a word of thanks for her efforts? A word, a teeny weeny word of acknowledgement? That was what she hated about men. It was not just the ingratitude. It was the fact that they never noticed dirt. They were dirty creatures. They would never wash if they could help it.

And she squeezed much too much washing-up liquid into the basin, and plunged her hands in, pummelling the water to work up a lather.

'You're a real water baby,' Frank said. Maybe if he kept his eyes open a bit longer, there'd be some sex. She seemed in all right form.

'Frank,' she said, very quietly. She was staring into the basin.

'Seen a ghost?' he said.

'I've cut the top off my finger,' she said in the same small voice. 'It must be in the basin. Under the suds.'

Frank peered into the basin, where her hands were still plunged.

'Take your hands out,' he said. He felt terribly strange.

'No,' she said. 'I can't, Frank. I don't want to see.'

Frank nudged the biggest bit of sud to one side with the wooden spoon. The water had discoloured, right enough. It was a sort of reddy shade.

'You nicked yourself,' he said.

Sheila had gone very white. Frank was afraid she might faint. He gripped her elbow, and pinched it. 'It's all right,' he kept saying.

Finally, he got her to lift her hands out. It was like bending a mannequin into shape in a shop-front window. Sheila had shut her eyes very tightly, and was biting her lower lip fiercely. She was rigid. The palp of the third finger on the right hand had been sliced off, almost to the moon of the nail.

'Christ Jesus,' Frank said. 'O, Christ Jesus.'

Sheila was shivering, her eyes shut like fists.

'Tell me,' she said. 'Tell me.'

Frank hammered his hands on the draining board as his lasagne came up. He clamped his mouth shut, and fluids ran from his nose. He began to choke.

'Frank,' Sheila cried. 'Take me to a hospital. Take me to a doctor.'

The keys to the car were in his pocket. He felt for them, found them. And the car? In the drive, he told himself, in the drive.

Sheila would not open her eyes. She held her hands in front of her, bunched. So he led her out, holding her wrist. The shivering had stopped. Her neck muscles were stiff with the determination to close her eyes and her mouth even more tightly. But the rest of her body was slack. Her steps were tired.

'Please open your eyes,' he said to her. 'Shutting your eyes will get us nowhere.'

He pulled open the car-door and half-forced, half-eased her into the seat. Now she had drawn her arms tightly against her, her good hand hiding her wounded hand. Her head ducked down.

'Go and get my finger,' she said. 'The doctors will sew it on for me. They do it all the time.'

This was a dream. This was not happening. Details were too real: the snail making foam on the tarmacadam, the moon making a lightning-bolt shimmy on the hood of the car, the wet glister on the snapdragons. In dreams you saw things clearly; in real life you didn't notice. You were going somewhere. Frank knew that in a moment, in a few moments maybe, he would feel Sheila's finger prodding his shoulder to wake him from his cat-nap at the butcher-block table. Then he would give out stink to her for getting flour on his jacket.

He tipped the basin, and began to drain off the water. Red trickled out with the suds and the water. All he could see was the egg-whisk, and the pastry cutter underneath it, and the Japanese knives. He picked up each instrument very slowly, as if there were trip-wires or fuses running from them. Then he moved his fingers, digit by digit, among the last few suds, looking straight ahead at the butter-yellow tiles on the wall.

He had touched something. Soggy, cold. His fingers walked around it, then touched it again. A teabag. His heart quietened. He was making too much adrenalin. This would kill him yet. That would be the last laugh.

When the tip of his nail grazed the edge of the finger-end, he tore off strips of kitchen-roll, and picked the thing up decisively. It must be it. There was nothing else in the basin except the teabag, and the least scrap of Brillo pad, like a tiny cutting of pubic hair. Even holding the kitchen-roll was enough. It was like swimming, when your feet glide against something slimy on the bottom.

'This is going to age me,' he said. 'This is going to put years on me.'

Damp was spreading through the paper layers.

She said nothing on the way to the hospital. She whimpered a little, but it was almost inaudible. Frank did not know whether to be glad or sorry that the traffic was heavy. He didn't fancy driving like a lunatic, or crashing lights. The police were all over the place. If the roads had been clear, she would have blamed him for not speeding. The least thing was grist to the mill. On balance, then, it was just as well that the roads were active. A finger would be the least of it if they hit some chap head-on.

'I accuse you,' Sheila said. 'I accuse you.'

In the Casualty Department, they treated her straight away. Sheila had calmed somewhat. Now her expression was far-away. She had opened her eyes and looked ahead vacantly. She was making no effort to hold back her shoulders, the way she usually did. Her breasts slumped heavily. The cavity between them deepened as she leaned forward. The skin above them was wrinkled, a little red. If she had been prepared, she would have worn a blouse instead of a V-neck cardigan; she would have worn a belt too. She had not even thought to change her house-shoes. It would have occurred to a thoughtful man, to someone who could cope. It would have.

Sheila looked at each of the two young doctors in the Casualty section. Did either of them find her the least bit attractive? If they had, they would have been more gentle, less business-like. She felt fat and dirty. She had been slicing onions that evening, and the smell was still on her arms. Her eyes were red from them. They would think she was not clean. That was the worst thing, worse even than the politeness of two young men who might have been her sons if she had been raped in puberty.

The nurses and doctors were swarming round her again. She let them do whatever they wanted to.

Frank could not believe the doctor.

'I read about it all the time,' he said. 'I read about whole hands being sewn back on. I remember hearing about a lumberjack who lost most of his arm in a saw-mill.'

'I'm afraid that sometimes television can give a false impression about things,' said the doctor.

'But I've read this in books,' Frank said.

'Books are not always truthful,' said the doctor.

Frank was dumbfounded.

'We can do a great deal,' the doctor said. 'Your wife is in shock. We can help her to absorb it. We can ensure that she sleeps comfortably tonight, here in the hospital. We can heal the wound. Afterwards, you can consider skin grafts, plastic surgery, that kind of thing. There are many options. The injury will not result in any loss of dexterity. It won't even be too unsightly.'

'She's very proud of her hands,' Frank said. This was not really so, but he felt that it might be the right thing to say.

The doctor gave as good as he got. 'Hands are wonderful things,' he said. 'They make you think.'

The people from Administration were taking a few details from Frank. Sheila was going into a semi-private room under a consultant with a Scottish-sounding name. A good night's rest would do her all the good in the world. She would be a different person in the morning. She would be herself again.

Now she was crying. Of course, it was understandable.

'I don't want part of me put in any incinerator,' she sobbed. 'Make them give it back to me.'

'They know best, sweetheart,' he said.

Sheila looked straight at him.

'I accuse you,' she said. 'I accuse you of mutilating me.'

Frank wished that the nurses would hurry up with the injection, or whatever it was they used. Sheila was understandable, but the whole thing was also very embarrassing. The doctors pretended to be busy about a hundred and one things, but you could bet your bottom dollar they had both ears open. They probably thought he had been fighting with her. They might even think that he had attacked her. Who knew what they were thinking?

He was relieved when they did sedate her. Her eyes did not roll back, the way that he had imagined they would; but her head lolled, and her voice became woozy.

'I point the finger of guilt at you,' she said. Her speech was slurred, her mouth dribbled water.

'She'll be better now,' the nurse said brightly. 'Poor thing.'

'We can make up a bed for you,' the Casualty Officer said to Frank. 'You probably want to stay with her.'

'I can't,' he said. 'I want to, but I can't. The house is open, the lights are on all over it, I forgot to put the spark-guard in front of the fire. It would be irresponsible not to go home.'

'You could ring your neighbours.'

'It would be unfair to disturb them at this hour,' Frank said. 'Besides, I have the housekeys.'

'I understand,' the Doctor said. 'Anyhow, you have no cause for anxiety. Your wife needs only to rest. A good night's beauty sleep works wonders. I'll pop in to see her early tomorrow morning.'

'I leave her in the best of hands,' Frank said.

In the hospital car-park, Frank sat with his head against the high wheel of his car, and felt a great need to cry. But it would be ridiculous to do so, he thought. There are other ways of coping with stress. For a time, he played with the headlights, moving the switch up and down, from dims to full and back again. He would not have said no to a cigarette. He was tempted to go to the kiosk in the hospital lobby and buy a packet. That would be the thin end of the wedge. Before he knew it, he would be puffing forty a day, and his two years' effort would be worth zilch.

Why did she go on like that? he wondered. What have I done wrong?

At home, he changed his mind about that drink. He needed one. Lemon or no lemon, he was going to have some kind of gin and tonic. Also, he was not about to traipse into the office the next day. No sirree. They could all go to hell.

Frank sat in the dark in his living-room, beside the gas cylinder. He lit two plaques and let the gin burn his mouth. What matter if he got a reflux? There were antacids somewhere. Anyhow, he felt like drinking the whole bottle.

'I do,' he said. 'I feel like drinking the whole bloody thing.'

Outside, way up in the night-sky, he could see the Milky Way. It was where it should be. It was doing its job. Below it, the backs of houses blocked out the trees in the park. They were not getting up to anything. They were doing what came naturally. In the morning, when the sun came up, that would be all right as well. It would slant between two particular branches on the walnut tree, and begin warming the seats in the car round about nine or nine-fifteen. The chrome on the car would glisten, because that was what it always did. If he had remembered to wipe it with a chamois the day before, it would glint even more. Because it was that kind of world. And there was nothing wrong with it being that way. If people were more honest, they would say so, instead of mooning around the place, poormouthing everything.

Where were those antacids anyway?

Frank had decided to finish the bottle. Ordinarily, he did not like getting drunk on his own; when he did, once in a blue moon, he left the lights on. He was not hiding from anyone. He had nothing to hide. But tonight was different. It was not every night that you looked up to find your wife had chopped off her finger. Small wonder if you acted accordingly.

After a while, Frank put on the third plaque of the gas cylinder. But it was no use. He was shivering all over.

PROPER NAMES

It HAD been a long lunch and a late one. If the truth were told, rather too much claret had been consumed; and the cigars, not that anyone was objecting, far exceeded the requirements of a midweek engagement. It was taking Henry all his time just to smoke his; and he was still somewhat confused and self-conscious about puncturing the wrong end with the cigar-piercer. The gaffe had made him talkative.

'Caught him out,' he said to the others. 'With his trousers down, you might say.'

The other two guffawed. Their attention had wandered. What on earth was the bloody chap talking about? Couldn't smoke a cigar, and held forth just the same, as if he owned the club.

'That's a great story, Henry,' they said.

The wine-waiter finally steeled himself for it.

'Gentlemen,' he said. 'I'm sorry for disturbing you.'

'That's all right, Jack,' said Henry's host. 'We accept your apologies.'

Guffaws. Henry wanted so much to shed his cigar. His hand stank.

'We have to set the tables for tonight,' said the wine-waiter. 'I'll have to ask you to take your port in the members' bar.'

'Rightio,' said the host. 'Henry will take you up, Pat. He knows where it is. I'll just slip out and sign the chit.'

But Henry did not know where the members' bar was. Why had he told that stupid lie about being there before? Why had he drunk so much claret? And why had he accepted this lion of a cigar? It was as thick as a hat-stand.

'I can't, old man,' he said, just like that. 'I must dash. I have people coming at four. I'll just get back in time.'

People respected abrupt departures, he told himself. He had read that in a psychology book.

'Rubbish,' said his host, using his height to make Henry seem puny. 'Keep them waiting. People respect people who keep them waiting.'

'Just show me where the members' bar is,' said Pat, beginning to suspect.

'Follow the smoke,' said Henry. Why did his face always let him down? He could feel it getting red.

The host was tired of embarrassing Henry. It was not worth it. It was lost on a little fellow like that, whatever kind of income he might have.

'I understand perfectly,' he said, putting a hand on Henry's shoulder. Even that was lost on a little man. 'You know your way out, old man.'

'I do,' said Henry.

'Of course you do,' his host said.

It was standing at the taxi-rank that Henry realized there was something wrong with his coat. The lining in the left pocket was not torn. It was tight under the shoulders. And there were buttons over the vent at the back. It was all very strange.

This is not my coat, he decided. But I shall not get excited about it. I shall not panic.

In the inside breast pocket, he found a wallet. No money, no cards. Two quite small keys, most likely for a briefcase. In the cellophane envelope, where a man might keep his photo-graph or that of his wife, or stamps, he could see grubby paper slips. The first was a receipt from a barber's salon called Hair Today; the second a green railway pass, three months expired, with exotic names written in pencil on the back: Speed of Sound, Volga, Espadrille.

Henry gingerly touched the muscles of his neck. The hairs were not spiky. Now he was certain. The wallet too belonged to another person. He had not been near a barber's shop. Besides, he couldn't remember taking a train anywhere in recent months. After all, he had a perfectly good car. Yet if that was indeed the case how did he come to be standing at a taxi-rank? Still, the writing on the rear of the railway pass was not his. His was precise, and tiny: it took him forever to fill up a postcard. And there was further evidence: the exotic names. Henry was no fool. He guessed they were the names of horses.

'And I,' he thought, 'have never been to a race-course in my life. I would not know where to find one.'

'You all right?' said the taxi-driver, who had pulled up beside him.

'I'm fine,' said Henry.

'Where to?' the cabby said.

'Nowhere,' Henry said. 'I have a perfectly fine car.'

Drunk, the cabby thought, and reversed the few yards to the elderly nun who had been afraid to stand beside Henry after he started talking to himself.

Henry felt strange, more strange than he had ever felt. What was the matter? Perhaps it was a simple matter of having had too much claret. He was a man who took sherry at Christmas, and wine at weddings. The claret, he decided, had been his downfall, not to speak of the cigar. That had been a downfall too.

A terrible possibility formed in his mind.

'I may have had a stroke,' he said. 'That would explain my confusion. It would throw light on my disorientation. Some ever so delicate tissue in my brain may have torn like paper. A blood clot, moping through my bloodstream, may have lodged at last in a warm recess of the cerebellum.'

Henry began reciting the alphabet. After that, he listed the Kings and Queens of Britain.

'My retentive powers are unimpaired,' he said. This was a comfort.

Yet the strangeness persisted.

'I may be having a heart-attack,' Henry said. 'That would deprive the brain of oxygen, and render me confused, or intermittent. I might be perfectly lucid about the Kings and Queens of Britain, yet quite unable to recall the disposition of light-switches in my own house.'

When the next taxi pulled up, Henry made up his mind on the spot. He would go straight home, and forget completely about the office. In his state, it would be much better to be at home, to be tucked in, to be mollycoddled and made much of. But by whom, he thought. By whom?

'Take me home, please,' he said.

The cabby could see at a glance that he was drunk.

'Where's home?' he said.

But Henry could not remember.

'Come on,' said the taxi-driver.

'I moved only last week,' Henry said. He was very embarrassed, and afraid. 'You know how it is if you move around all the time. In the diplomatic corps, I mean.'

'Lost your left oar, mate?' And the cabby shot forward twenty feet to where a housewife was absolutely laden down with hatboxes and shoeboxes.

'I must have a home,' Henry said. 'Everybody does.'

There was a kind of greeny red at the corner of his field of vision. Little strings of colour whipped around like snakes.

'How did I get here?' Henry cried.

A third taxi drew up. The cabby flung open the door. Music exploded in the compartment. The percussion was like a heartbeat.

'Where to?' said the cabby, who was young, and had eyebrow pencil in the blond hairs of his first moustache. His fingers kept time on the steering wheel.

'Take me to a hospital,' Henry said. 'I am not myself.'

The nurses were nice, in a brisk way. But the queue seemed to take forever. The people sitting beside Henry looked straight ahead into the middle distances. Accident and Emergency Departments are full of middle distances. People sitting there stare into them like they were fires, or the sea. Henry looked into them too, but he could see nothing. Across from him, a fourteen-year-old boy without any spots was leafing through *Town and Country* with his finger stuck in a page toward the middle. He kept coming back to it. He would look at the page very quickly, with his head down, then turn again to browse through the small-print property pages.

'Won't be long now,' said the nurse.

'Are you talking to me?' Henry said.

'Who else?' She was a little hurt. She had meant well.

Henry could not sit still. He walked up and down the corridor of the Casualty Department, feeling very tight and sticky under his arms. But perhaps the coat was his. Perhaps it had shrunk at the dry-cleaners. Was that possible? If it were, then perhaps he had had the coat darned and buttoned for a consideration by someone working at the dry-cleaners, or maybe the laundrette. Right now, he was not in a position to know. He was, if you like, lost. But everything would be clear to him in due course. He would live to make light of this.

Names were called, and people got up without looking at anyone, when theirs was shouted. But how would Henry know when to answer? What name would they call him by? Would they call him 'Sir', or would they call him Mr Other, the way coaches did when a football team was one short, and the extra player was called A.N. Other? Surely they were well used by now to treating people who could not provide them with names, either because they were in a coma or because they were confused.

'If I think of something else,' Henry said, 'my name will come back to me. If I think of other names, I will hit on my own. After that, I can start to find my second name. When I get that far, I will be home and dry.'

He started at A, which was logical.

'Alan,' he said, 'Anthony, Arthur.'

But it was none of those. It could not be Adam either. Nobody called their children Adam, not even Jews.

'Gangway,' said the porter wheeling the trolley with the covered body.

Henry stood aside.

'Ask me a name,' he said.

The porter looked at him closely.

'You all right, Dad?' he said.

From the curtained cubicle at the other end of the corridor, somebody started screaming.

'Ask me a name,' Henry said. 'A name with B.'

'What you need,' said the porter, kicking the brake off the trolley as he pushed it forward, 'is a nice hot cup of tea.'

'Brian is not it,' said Henry. 'I thought of Brian.'

'Your name?' said the Casualty Officer. He was a pleasant

young man, with the mark of two rings on his tanned fingers. Perhaps he was just back from his honeymoon. That would explain the rings – one signet, one wedding – and the tan. I am going to be all right, thought Henry. I have a sharp mind.

'It's a blank,' said Henry.

'Not to worry,' the Casualty Officer said. 'I forget mine too. All the time.'

'Do you know it just now?' Henry asked. The colours at the corners of his eyes were still there, but they were wavering now instead of writhing. Their brightness had eased.

'Let's find out yours first,' said the doctor. 'Then we can talk about mine.'

'I am not myself,' said Henry. 'I have not been myself for hours.'

'Does your wife know where you are?' The doctor began to take notes.

'I don't know if I have a wife,' Henry said. The colours had started up again. He raised his hand to brush them away.

'Would you prefer to forget?' said the doctor. 'If you had the choice, would you rather be single or married?'

'I would rather be made much of,' said Henry. Three cubicles down, the screaming renewed.

'He would rather be single,' said the doctor as he wrote something down.

'Ask me a D name,' Henry said. He had got that far.

'David,' said the doctor. Where in the name of God was Ahad? Ahad was on at seven; it was seven-ten already. Pakistanis were all the same. Apples fall near their tree. You can't change a leopard's spots.

'David is not it,' said Henry. 'Daniel is not it either. Anyhow, it would not be a Jewish name. I feel I could not be Jewish.'

'You look like a David to me,' said the doctor. 'You have a Davidy look about you.'

It just wasn't fair that he had to sit here with a drunk. Jesus Christ, where was Ahad? Enough was enough.

'Doctor,' he said, disgustedly.

'Doctor is not it either,' said Henry. 'Since when was Doctor a name?'

It was probably Ahad. Anyhow, he was black. Even without the stethoscope, his white coat was sufficient to denominate him.

'How does your wife feel about your drinking?' he asked Henry. His tone was very gentle.

Henry looked at him.

'I even know the Anglo-Saxon Kings, or most of them,' he said. 'Why does my own name elude me?'

'Do you want to stop drinking?' said Doctor Ahad. 'Do you feel any motivation?'

Henry began to cry. He cried without making any noise.

'I want to give myself a name,' he said. 'I do not want to be anonymous.'

'Are you on anti-depressants too?' Doctor Ahad said. His manner was as gentle as ever. 'That would explain your confusion. The two do not mix. To combine them would be injudicious.'

'Dr Ahad,' Henry said. 'You seem . . .'

'How did you know my name?' said the doctor. He was quite alarmed.

'It was a lucky guess,' Henry said. 'You seem a very kind man. Would you humour me for a while? Would you ask me names beginning with E and F? I put them together because it strikes me that there are few names which begin with E, and many of them would be women's names. I appreciate that the request may strike you as whimsical, but I know it would help me.'

'Why not?' Dr Ahad said. 'Just leave my name out of it.'

'I have already been through Ernest, Eugene, and Evan,' Henry said. 'It it none of those.'

'I think you've been bold,' the doctor said, wagging a finger at Henry. 'I think you've been doctoring your drinkie-poos with pills.'

Round half past eight Henry started crying again. It was much less fun when he did that. Dr Ahad had been fascinated by him till then. He was thinking of doing his membership in Psychiatry instead of going on the three-year Medical Roster, and Henry's case presented a striking example of the borderland between neurophysiology and psychopathology, or, more colloquially, between genes and bonkers. There was a thesis, maybe a book, in that area. So the doctor wandered off in search of his friend, the Senior House Officer in Surgery, who was from Qatar, and had perfectly trimmed fingernails. He found him in the canteen, squeezing two chicken portions and a bowl of crab soup into the microwave.

'Come see the first drunk of the evening,' Dr Ahad said.

'One drunk is much like another,' said his friend.

'But this one is an almost perfect representative of Korsakov's Syndrome. You could wheel him into a lecture. He is the funniest.'

'You should not joke about suffering, Ahad. Making a living is a serious business.'

Still, the Senior House Officer went to have a look. The two men found Henry sitting on the middle part of the camp-bed in the cubicle. He had finally agreed to take off his shoes, but no one could persuade him to part with the coat he was wearing.

'I am onto G,' he said to them.

His face was swollen with tears and shame.

The Senior House Officer decided to try the Socratic method.

'Are you afraid of dying?' he said to Henry.

'I think I am,' Henry said. 'I am always afraid when I hear an ambulance. I should cut down on salt, but I find the flesh is weak. At night, I leave a light burning.'

'Do you believe in a God?' said the Senior House Officer.

'I don't know,' Henry said. 'I want to, but then I hear about orphanages burning down. On the other hand, who straightened the spine? How did we learn to walk upright? I am always meaning to read the Bible properly.'

Dr Ahad had got the hang of it.

'So this is the Socratic method?' he said.

'It takes time,' his friend said, 'but you get there in the end.'

'If you were very frightened,' Dr Ahad said to Henry, 'would you prefer to be hugged by me or the nurse who showed you in?'

'The nurse,' Henry said. 'At the same time, I have nothing against coloured persons.'

'So now we know,' said Dr Ahad excitedly, 'that you are afraid of dying, you believe in God from time to time but not all the time, and you like girls. You are existential, you are agnostic, and you are heterosexual.'

'You see how easy it is?' said his friend. 'Have another go.'

'It's your turn,' Dr Ahad said.

'Do you know the names of the last five English monarchs?' said the Senior House Officer to Henry.

'Of course I do,' said Henry. 'It is my own name that eludes me.'

'But now we know that you are middle-class,' said Dr Ahad. 'Only a middle-class person would say "elude".'

'I don't say "elude",' said his friend, 'and I am the son of a wealthy manufacturer.'

Dr Ahad was enchanted.

'The Socratic method could revolutionize the whole treatment of post-traumatic stress syndrome,' he said. 'Amnesia could be treated logotherapeutically instead of chemotherapeutically.'

'Henry!' cried Henry.

'What are you talking about?' said the Senior House Officer.

'I have found my name,' Henry said. 'It was when you talked about the Royal Line in England. I remembered Harold, and then Henry. Henry the Eighth.'

'How wonderful,' said Dr Ahad. 'I have heard Julius Caesar, I have heard William Shakespeare, I have heard Jesus Christ, but never Henry the VIII.'

'I have had a William the Conqueror,' said the Senior House Officer. 'He was a nice guy.'

Henry had completely broken down. It was a bit disgusting, however much you liked him.

'I don't know how to thank you,' he said, sobbing. 'I don't know how to express my gratitude. I had begun to feel as if I were a monster. In all my life, I have never experienced such a sensation of unnaturalness.'

'There is nothing to be ashamed of,' said the Senior House Officer. 'You are a very natural person. It happens to everybody. Most people keep their name on something close by them to cope with this kind of contingency. I wake up at night sometimes, and I don't know who I am. The important thing is, never panic.'

'This is ordinary?' Henry said. 'This is usual?'

'This is our daily grind,' said Dr Ahad's friend. 'Our daily bread.'

'You are abnormally normal,' Dr Ahad said. 'You are very average. Your height is average, your appearance is average, your problem-solving skills are average. You have no distinguishing features.'

'You certainly know a lot of names,' the Senior House Officer said. 'I have never heard so many personal names.'

'So many Christian names,' Dr Ahad corrected him.

'I have always liked names,' Henry said. He was beginning to feel shy.

'Now you have everything a man could want,' Dr Ahad said.

'I have no home to go to,' said Henry.

'I suspect,' said the Senior House Officer, holding up a finger, 'that we might be able to determine a probable fixed address for our friend here. I would not be taken aback, still less would I be surprised, if it transpired that an address was printed, picked out, or inked, on the cloth material of his inside coat pocket.'

And it was so.

Henry sat shamefacedly on the camp-bed while the two doctors looked him over rather strictly. They had every right to, he thought. There was little point in telling them about the railway pass, or the barber's receipt, or the stitched pockets, or the buttoned vents.

'My God,' said the Senior House Officer in horror.

Henry had to meet his eyes.

'The microwave,' said Dr Ahad's friend. 'I forgot the microwave.'

Henry felt in his pocket for a housekey, but of course there was none. So he rang the buzzer, and stood waiting, listening to rainwater drip from the rhododendrons. Inside, a light went on; then another. He could hear someone taking off the chain.

The door opened. A woman in a lavender dressing-gown looked at him without speaking. Behind him, he could hear the taxi reverse on the grass verge, then back onto the gravel.

'I am home,' he said.

'What kind of a person are you?' the woman said.

He peered at her closely. She was a perfect stranger to him, yet he felt he should know her.

'So tell me,' the woman said. 'What sort of man are you? How can you do these things to me? Who do you think you are? Who do you think you are, anyway?'

Henry sensed that he was not steady on his feet. He bent his head. The greeny red came at him from both sides.

'It's not William,' he said. 'Or Wilfrid. Nobody calls anyone Wilfrid nowadays. Walter is rare.'

'Why are you doing this?' the woman said.

'Ask me a name,' he said. 'Ask me one beginning with X.'

IN THE DARK

THE LIGHTS had gone out all over the O Muirithe household, and Harry and Joan were obliged to talk to one another. At the end of a difficult day, this was the last straw. Indeed, it was the short one. After all, they had been married for twenty-seven years, and were naturally speechless.

'The bastards,' said Harry. 'The bloody bastards. They said eight o'clock. They swore it.'

'I know,' said Joan. 'I know they did.'

'Zone B. No risk after eight. You can't believe daylight out of them.'

'It's only ten past.'

'I tell you this,' said Harry. 'The next house we buy, it's going to be . . .'

'Within spitting distance of a hospital,' said Joan.

'Within spitting distance,' said Harry. 'So near, so close you can hear the doctors putting in stitches, and the static on the set in the television lounge of the geriatric ward.'

(Harry had been to visit his father once when the old man became prematurely senile and had spent was it four years in just such an institution, rambling on about the toy-train in the park and the baby wallabies in the zoo sticking their heads out of their mother's pouches; but it was the static on the set which had always angered his son to the point where he had walked away in a pet. This, by the way, is a digression, the first of four, and you are quite at liberty to ignore them utterly. For my own part, I shall play fair, and indicate each one by the use of the parenthesis.)

'. . . of the geriatric ward.'

'And the nurses at their tea-break,' said Joan.

'And the nurses at their tea-break,' said Harry. 'Scraping out the last bit of strawberry yoghurt.'

'Next year,' said Joan.

'Next year,' Harry said.

There was a long silence. The battery clock on the mantelpiece ticked, as battery clocks do; and the curtains stirred, but only slightly.

'I could light a fire.'

But that was typical of Joan: trying to look on the bright side.

'I wouldn't bother.'

'Not for the heat. For the light. It'd be nice for Johnny and Avril.'

'You wouldn't see your nose under the stairs. You'd crack your skull open.'

Joan was hurt by this. Not that she noticed. She was as used to being hurt as to being fifty.

'I would have missed my bus if I'd stayed to set it,' she said. 'I had to be out by eight.'

'Am I complaining? Have I uttered a single syllable of re-crimination? You shouldn't have to set it. Let Johnny set it.'

'You try asking Johnny to set it. Set it, my foot. Johnny wouldn't even know how to roll a newspaper.'

'Don't ask him. Tell him. Order him. Asking gets you nowhere. Telling gets you nowhere. This world is about the boot. Get the boot in. Look, where are those other candles? These two are useless. They're wobbly. They'd set the whole place on fire. You have to soften the bottom ends first. Soften the bottom end of one of them with the flame off the other. Then you sort of wedge it into the saucer till the wax hardens again. Are you with me?'

'I'm not a fool,' Joan said. 'Don't talk to me as if I were a fool.'

'I'm not saying you're a fool. I'm not suggesting you're a fool. I'd never have thought of going to the church. I thought the candles were electric nowadays. At least they were the last time I was there. So you did well. I hand it to you.'

'Now you're patronizing me,' Joan said. 'Please don't patronize me.'

Harry had meant well. He had meant well and he had been misunderstood. It was the story of his life. The story of his life could be summed up in the one word 'misunderstanding'. But he would be patient. He would not retaliate. 'Have you taken your Melleril?' he asked gently. 'Or did you forget again?' And then, before Joan could answer, he was noisily rummaging among the remaining candles.

'Here,' he said. 'What about this one?'

'What one?'

'Here. Where's your hand? That one.'

Joan smelled it.

'Harry, it's that awful scented kind. I can't stand them.'

'But it'll give us more light. And we need more light. Those piddly ones are for shrines.'

'The shrine of St Jude,' Joan said, which was, all considered, an excellent riposte; that is, if you know your saints, and Harry didn't. But it was still worth saying, and I personally regard it as a high point in the story. Harry lit a match. It struck the third time round, lighting their faces in a quite uncomplimentary fashion, and filling the room with their shadows.

'Harry, that scented smell makes me sick,' said Joan.

'Well, I'm not just going to squat here in total darkness. I've been working since I woke up. Surely to Christ I can . . .'

'I've been working too,' said Joan. 'Ever since I came in from work I've been working. I did the washing by hand. I went out again, to get the candles. In the rain.'

'Violins,' said Harry softly. 'Violins.'

'This is just hell. They never strike when it's summer. They do it when it gets dark.'

Harry had moved quietly out of the small circle of light in which she was sitting. He knew perfectly well why he was doing it too, but it was not revenge. It was a matter of principle. He still felt misunderstood.

'Harry? Harry? Where are you?'

'Nigeria,' he said. 'Where do you think I am?'

'Are you sure you're all right?'

Harry managed a small wheeze. He even tried to prolong it, but his lungs were clear. In any event, it achieved the desired effect.

'Are you breathless?'

'A bit. A bit breathless. It'll pass.'

'Sit down, Harry. Sit down and hold your head in your hands.'

(Harry's father had died on a ventilator, and Harry had persuaded Joan that the ailment was hereditary. He had almost persuaded himself. Ventolin inhalers were scattered strategically round about the whole house, and they served to inhibit outbreaks of marital discord. After all, Harry might not be here tomorrow, and words spoken in wrath might well be regretted. It was still only five years since her husband had taken the bus from the funeral parlour to add to the pathos of his father's removal, and had sat staring at 'Charley's Angels' without uttering a sentence, letting the barbecue chicken grow cold on his lap: Joan had forgotten none of this, and was easily panicked.)

'. . . and hold your head in your hands.'

'I am holding my head in my hands.'

'When do you think we'll have light, Harry?'

'When we reach the end of the tunnel. And not before.'

'This is hell.'

There was a long silence. The battery clock on the mantelpiece was still ticking; and the curtains stirred, but only slightly.

'What we need,' Harry decided, 'is someone like Mussolini. Benito would have known what to do. Line up the ringleaders. Shoot 'em down. Finito. That's the only thing that would bring these fellows to their senses. Make them tighten their belts. Both barrels. No bloody strikes in those days.'

Joan was relieved. Harry hadn't wheezed once.

'I wouldn't mind if they were paid badly,' she said.

'Yes, sirree,' Harry said. 'There's a lot to be said for a man like Mussolini.'

'You're just cross because you're missing your programme.'

'I was waiting for that,' said Harry.

'I don't know why you race home to watch that eejit.'

'I don't race anywhere. I haven't the energy. I work too hard.'

'And he's not even funny,' said Joan.

'My God, if I had to choose between Benny Hill and . . . and Mother Teresa, I know who I'd plumb for.'

'Just bottoms and sniggers,' she said. 'And the two of you sitting there, tittering. You're as bad as Johnny.'

'I've made up my mind,' said Harry, who hadn't. 'I *am* going to smoke.'

'You can't, Harry. Not now. Not after three weeks.'

'I can't have a hot meal,' Harry said. 'I can't watch Benny Hill. I can't have a normal conversation about normal things. The least I can do is smoke myself silly.'

'You mustn't give in.'

'Give me one good reason.'

'You'll live longer.'

'Jesus Christ,' said Harry with a ferocity which almost surprised him. 'That's the best bloody reason for taking them up.'

Noise in the hallway startled Joan.

'Harry, stop it, they're coming. And make an effort for me. Don't call her Shelley. Please. It's very unkind.'

But Harry was not about to lower his voice.

'Well, I liked Shelley. She was good for Johnny. Besides, she was a doctor. This one's a nurse. Next time round, I suppose he'll be dating the porter.'

Johnny's voice called out from the darkness of the doorway.

'Dr and Mrs Livingstone, I presume?'

Then Avril's, more timidly.

'Hello, Mr O Moorithe.'

'Shelley,' Harry said.

'Avril,' she replied. The girl was obviously dense: there wasn't a hint of malice in her voice.

'Force of habit,' Harry said to the darkness. 'Mea culpa.'

'Don't mind my Pater, Avril,' Johnny said. 'His nerves are shot. He's off the fags.'

But Avril ignored him. Shelley would have shown more spunk.

'Hi, Mrs O Moorithe.'

'Hello, love. Mind where you stand. I have a tray on the floor somewhere.'

'I can't stand the way she says it,' Harry said to Johnny in an audible undertone. 'O Moorithe. Can you not get her to pronounce it the right way? Shelley never had any difficulty, but then Shelley . . .'

'It has to do with the way you part your lips,' Johnny said. 'I'll work on it later.'

(Johnny was not ordinarily insolent; indeed, he lacked a capacity to do otherwise than dislike his father, a circumstance which chose him for this fiction, since in fiction the facts must fit that fabulous domain we poormouth as the ordinary world. But he'd been studying late in the National Library, and Avril had arrived to collect him at least an hour after the agreed time. He had pretended irritation, feeling little if any; so Avril had told him that, later in the evening, she would dress in her nurse's uniform and allow him to spank her across his lap with a rolled-up newspaper. He had had an erection ever since, and feared no one, not even his father.)

'Isn't this gas?' said Avril to Joan. 'I bet there'll be tons of babies in nine months time.'

'Don't be putting ideas in his head,' Joan said. But she liked Avril; it was a feminine thought and, besides, the girl worked, or had once worked, in the neo-natal unit.

There was a long silence. The battery clock could not prevent itself ticking gently and gingerly; and the curtains stirred in the lightest of breezes.

'You could have set a fire,' said Johnny.

'You could have set one,' said Joan. The darkness made her confident.

'Missed your programme, Dad?'

But Harry ignored him.

'I tell you this for nothing, Avril. I don't know how you feel, but I was saying to Johnny's mother that Mussolini had the right idea.'

'What was that?' said Avril.

'My father is about to deliver himself of a political apophthegm,' said Johnny. 'Stand well clear.'

'Johnny's father is just being difficult,' said Joan.

'What is that dreadful smell?' said Johnny, sniffing the darkness.

'I think it's lovely,' Avril said. 'I think it's churchy, sort of.'

'Bring in the troops,' Harry said. 'Pick four men at random. You, you, you, you. Out to the factory gates. Bayonet practice. Now that's my kind of crash course in industrial relations.'

'More crash than course,' said Johnny.

But Avril disagreed.

'I think it's a wonderful idea, Mr O Moorithe. After all, the working classes are getting ideas above their station. They think they can hold the country up to ransom.'

'How right you are, Avril,' Harry said warmly. 'How right you are.'

'But wouldn't it be a better idea to cut off their arms and legs first?'

(Avril was no more impudent than Johnny. I have known her a long time and have always found her to be easily cowed and crestfallen, with a complex of sorts about her skin, which is so fair it tans badly even with minimal exposure on the sunbed in the solarium. But that very afternoon she had been taking a quite handsome patient's blood pressure in the Admission Ward, and the back of his hand had grazed against the watch strap which she wore on her left breast. It was only a moment, a matter of seconds. But it had been deliberate. Of that she was sure. And the surety solaced her.)

'Well,' said Harry, managing another slight wheeze. 'That puts me in my place, doesn't it?'

The silence lengthened like a strip of chewing-gum between a child's fingers. The battery clock went on ticking with a desperate self-consciousness, like a man breaking wind in company; and the curtains twitched, but only just.

'I'll put . . . the kettle on,' said Joan.

'Momma,' Johnny said. 'No electricity. Ergo, no tea.'

'I wasn't thinking. I must be . . . tired.'

'We should be going,' Avril said. She was sorry now.

'And let the two of you get back to . . . to . . .' said Johnny, whose erection was beginning to subside.

'We were just chatting,' said Harry.

'We were . . . reminiscing,' Joan said.

'That's the great thing about power cuts,' said Harry. 'They give you time to talk. You're not just sitting like a zombie in front of the goggle box. And when you go to bed, you can't even remember what you were watching. No, your mother and I were talking. Looking back. There's so much to look back at. And to look forward to, of course.'

'We were remembering your blanket, Johnny. Johnny had a blanket, Avril. He was only a toddler at the time. People kept showering him with toys, you know the sort of cuddly bears people buy. But he couldn't be bothered with any of them. All he wanted was his dirty old blanket. He wouldn't sleep without it. He even took it to Montessori in his satchel.'

'And the games he used to play,' said Harry. 'With his marbles and his toy soldiers. He'd line them up at one end of the room and aim at them with his marble from the other end. You should have seen the skirting board. Chips here, chips there, chips everywhere. Great years. The best years. We were looking back . . . at it all.'

'You can spend hours . . . looking back,' said Joan.

'Ages. A lifetime.'

'We didn't even notice it was getting . . .'

'Dark all around us.'

'We were so engrossed,' Joan said.

Johnny was furious. Furious, yet contrite too. His erection had collapsed.

'Well,' he said, 'we don't want to break up the party. Or is it a seance?' Blankets and marbles. How could they do this to him? And what chance was there now of Avril's stretching herself across his lap in her nurse's uniform? Bugger all. She would want to talk about his childhood.

'Tell him off, Mrs O Moorithe,' Avril said. 'He needs a good clip on his ear.'

'Your predecessor set a high standard when it came to that sort of thing,' Harry said.

'Pater,' said Johnny, 'missing Benny Hill is no excuse for rudeness.'

'Do you watch Benny Hill, Mr O Moorithe?' said Avril.

'Who,' he replied, 'is Benny Hill?'

'Oh, you'd love him. He's a panic. A bit saucy, but he makes you laugh. Johnny says he's a dirty old man, but I like him.'

Harry decided Avril was all right. But Johnny's despair had deepened.

'What are we doing here, standing in the darkness?' he said.

'Power cuts make you queer,' his mother said.

'Andiamo,' Johnny decided. 'Avril Airlines announce a flight departure.'

'Where are you off to?' Harry said. He wanted Avril to go on talking about Benny Hill. In a strange way, he found it rather arousing.

'We're off to *The Seventh Heaven*,' Johnny said.

'I'd go there like a shot if I knew where to find it,' said Harry.

'I should have rang my folks,' Avril said.

'Ring from the club.'

'Stay a bit,' Harry said. 'It's early. Please.'

'Sure what's your hurry?' Joan said.

The truth is, Harry was a little afraid of being left alone with Joan. Why had she started all that nonsense about blankets and cuddly toys? And Joan was a little more than afraid of being left alone with Harry. By now, the ice-cubes would have melted in the freezer, and Harry hated his whiskey without at least three ice-cubes.

'There'll be lights any minute now,' said Harry. 'You'll see. You could even watch that programme you were talking about.'

But Johnny stood his ground.

'Adieu, farewell, remember us.'

'I suppose I'd better . . .' Avril said.

'Do stay,' said Joan. And she prayed for the lights to come on; she prayed against the darkness which was so bewildering.

'A firm and final Ciao,' Johnny said. It delighted him to hear his parents begging. Openly begging. His erection began to stir again.

'Wear your safety belts,' his father said, giving up and giving in.

'We'll take every precaution,' Johnny said. He could get a newspaper at the corner shop. Unless it were closed because of the power cut. Anyhow, there were dozens of newsagents along the route to the club.

'See you,' said Avril, who had seen neither of them.

'That's right,' Johnny said. 'We'll see you in a different light in future.'

And the two of them left, just like that.

When the hall door slammed shut, there was a short silence. I am not going to talk about the battery clock or the curtains because that point has been well and truly established, and you can imagine it for yourself. After all, we are in this together.

'So,' said Joan.

'Well?'

'Hmm?'

'Nothing,' said Harry.

'Nice child.'

'I should have rang.'

'Who?' said Joan.

'Rang. It's wrong. It should be rung.'

'What?'

'Never mind.'

He had not thought of the whiskey or the ice-cubes yet. Perhaps there was still time.

'She's very confident,' Joan said.

'I like her.'

'That's a bit of a U-turn.'

'She's very . . . feminine.'

Joan was thunderstruck. Harry had always doted on Shelley, though he tended to mistake her surname and call her Winters instead of Brennan.

'Is there a full moon tonight?' she asked him.

Harry came clean. One tends to do that in the darkness.

'I liked what she said about Benny Hill. It was natural.'

'I think we're all going mad,' Joan said.

But Harry had made up his mind, the way Joan made up her face: slowly and deliberately.

'Yes,' he said. 'She's more natural than Shelley.'

It was more than a decision. It was a conviction. Harry felt he owed himself a drink. A double, at that. And why not? Who was there to see? So he edged along the sofa in the general direction of the kitchen.

'Damn it, damn it, Harry, look at that! You've knocked the candle! It must have dripped wax all over the carpet.'

'So what?' said Harry. 'It'll come off.'

'It'll come off? All on its ownie own, I suppose?'

'Would you ever calm down?' Harry shouted.

'It won't just "come off",' Joan sobbed. 'I'll get it off. On my hands and knees, that's how.'

'Isn't there a pill you could take?' said Harry. He had just remembered that the freezer would be off and the ice-cubes melted. What was a whiskey without an ice-cube? A gin without a tonic, that was what.

'And it stinks the whole house,' Joan said. She was weeping now. It was so bloody typical. She made the effort for strangers. For her own husband it was a different matter. All hell broke loose once the hall door heaved to.

'Blankets,' Harry spat. 'What in Christ's name were you doing talking about blankets?'

'You were worse,' she wept. 'You were worse with your marbles.'

'Eight o'clock,' Harry said between clenched teeth. 'Eight o'clock. The bastards. They said eight o'clock we'd be out of danger.'

'I know,' Joan shouted at him. 'I know.'

'Mussolini was right. Shoot every last manjack. To hell with them. To hell with the whole lot of them.'

And the lights came on. Delicate white lace curtains blew in the air of the open window; and from the kitchen, above the hum of the peach-coloured fridge, Harry and Joan could hear the fragile sound of the battery clock, with a noise like matchsticks breaking. For a brief moment, husband and wife looked at each other: the man with the stained moustache and the tiny crack in the lens of his spectacles; the woman in her housecoat with needle and thread stuck into the linen lapel, and the bright, brown hair with grey at its roots. For as long as the moment lasted, they longed for the darkness. But it passed, as all unendurable things must. Light was one thing, illumination another. That was a word to be kept strictly for Christmas.

'Well, glory be,' said Joan.

'The power of prayer,' said Harry.

'Just like that.'

'All's well that ends well.'

'I'd better go round the house,' said Joan anxiously. 'I left lights on all over the place.'

'May light perpetual shine upon us!' said Harry. It would only take an hour or so for the cubes to congeal again. 'What time is it?'

'Ten to nine,' said Joan.

'Goodo. I'll get the last ten minutes of Benny Hill. And there's Dallas at ten. Is it tonight is Dallas night?'

'Don't you know well it is?'

'We're set so. Crisis averted.'

'Right as rain.'

'Right as rain,' Harry agreed.

'High and dry,' said Joan, as she turned off the overhead light and one of the side-lamps.

'High and dry,' Harry repeated. 'Or is it home and dry? I'm always getting the two of them mixed up.'

Joan banged the window shut, and the curtains stood stock-still. Harry was pressing the buttons on the television remote control. The noise of the stations swelled above the sound of the battery clock.

LATE AT NIGHT IN THE STANFORD LIBRARY

HE HAD been watching her since she came in. But this in itself was not remarkable. He had done the same thing, the one thing, each night for three weeks now. Had she been flighty, his work would have been cut out. Other girls were capricious, unpunctual; but she had a routine, and she abided by it. So long as he had arrived by seven-thirty, he would have time to mount up a stack of books, to open and close a wire-spine folder, to make occasional notes on the blond department stationery, and to coil the rubber bands around his wrist as he pulled them off the rolled batches of term papers he had to grade for the Pre-Socratic course. At eight sharp, she arrived; at eight-five, she was lost to him, the soft wash of legal paper nursing her elbows at either side.

Acknowledge me, he would think. Acknowledge me.

But she never turned her head. Others might bend spoons, wither flowers, crack suspension bridges, open up fissures in the earth. He could not persuade one dark-haired sophomore to turn upon him her large, incredulous eyes. For all that he concentrated his attentiveness and desire; for all that he remained there, night after night and this the twenty-first, one desk away from her. It was too bad.

Yet there was still time. It was early days.

This much he had discovered, almost from the first day. Her name was Sandra Solomons; she was a student of English and Human Biology, but she had registered as Pre-Medical; she had a sibling, a brother; she was rooming off campus in a house on Cowper; she loved the smell of eucalyptus. When she studied, she would stroke her knees, trousered or bare, her mouth a little open, not too much.

This was something. Much might be deduced from it. Even if this were not so, the manner in which he had arrived at this information made him feel at one with her, a protective presence near at hand in case of need. He had stood next to her at the check-out, leaving the library that first night of high August. She had six, perhaps seven, books in the crook of her bare arms; he hoped she might drop them. What better way to meet? But she balanced them fairly, piling them in a rush on the counter.

'Limit of four on Undergraduate borrowings,' said the black assistant.

'Does that mean I must leave three?' she said.

'You can count,' the black assistant said brightly.

So she took out *Seven Types of Ambiguity*, *God our Mother*, and *My Road to Zen*, by Percy Brennan, SJ.

'These can wait,' she said, and he watched her writing slipcards for the others. There it was. Sandra Solomon. Or Solomons? Or Sandy? He had heard Sandy a few times.

'Thank you, Mrs Bookworm Solomons.'

She laughed at that, showing the pink tip of her tongue. When she turned away and passed him, there was a frail slipstream of her toilet-water. He watched her run down the wide, curving staircase, one arm out for balance, the other gripping her backpack.

The black librarian was looking at her too.

Yet he never saw her with anyone. Twice a day perhaps, he caught a glimpse of her in the coffee-house. Then he would try to manoeuvre his way towards her through the crowd. While she picked out her lunch, he would stand beside her, anxiously inspecting a peach for bruises, or poking among the croissants in search of one with chocolate on it, although he knew that this line had been discontinued at the patisserie.

Her own diet was regular. She went for the plain yoghurts and, sometimes, for a pineapple variety. A slice of cheese, some rather blackish bread the purists ate, a little mayonnaise, and Perrier water, left open a long while before she drank it. Every so often, she would throw in a piece of cherry cake, or almond cake. And why not? She was thin, even anorexic, round the waist, though when she sat, her bottom filled out a bit. He would always sit two or three tables down from her while she ate, but she rarely looked around, even when the odd tray was dropped or the coffee-maker hissed swiftly, and steamed up the South East Asian corner. No, she would go at it, hunched and head down, straightening only when her meal was finished, and she treated herself to a Winston, tapping the smoke against the soft packet and working the bent end smooth between her fingers. That was because she went around with the packet in her hip-pocket.

Once he almost got involved.

'Two bagels, one and forty. Perrier, one and ten; bread, forty. Coffee – is that the special?'

'No,' she said. 'It's the house coffee.'

'Thirty-five. And the peach, thirty-five. The yoghurt, eighty. That makes four dollars forty.'

'Are you sure?' she said, counting her quarters from one hand into the other.

'I'm not sure of anything,' said the girl on the register. 'But the machine is.'

'Can I help you over here, sir?' said the young man at the next check-out.

No, damn you, no.

'I've got it,' she said happily, handing over a fistful of change. 'You've cleaned me out.'

Shit. Why didn't he just say 'Put it on mine.' But she would have hated that. She was probably feminist.

'You get to keep the food anyway,' the teller said to her.

Or he could have said 'Can I help?' No one could mind that. Not in public, in broad daylight.

'Two dollars even,' the teller said.

He looked at her vacantly.

Another time. Almost a week after he had first seen her in the library, he saw her in the bookstore, on her hunkers and twisted to one side. Her shorts stretched way up her thigh, high over the tan-mark. Her feet were bare, the soles very black. She was moving a finger, title by title, along the lowest shelf in the Art History section. She had reached M, and was hovering there.

Monet, he thought. Manet, Michelangelo. Mandrian. Or was it Mondrian?

'I guess we're taking the same course. Are you a friend of Rudy's?'

No. That had neither style nor surprise.

'Have you seen Frankelburger on Michelangelo?'

But maybe she knew the whole Michelangelo scene.

'Have you come across Torsakoff on *Semiosis and Middle Manet* in your travels along that shelf?'

Pretentious? Preppie?

'Sandra. Sandra Solomons.'

'Sally. Sally Donovan.'

'How *are* you?'

'How are *you*?'

'Fine. Just fine.'

'Me too.'

'Checking out a book?'

'If I find it.'

'Happy hunting, Sandra.'

'You too, Sally.'

She stood, straightened, bent. Sweet God, what legs. A wee strand of pubic hair peeked round the edge of her sun-shorts. Skin had peeled – in the bath, perhaps? – from her ankles. The backs of them were quite pale; but her calves and thighs were deep brown, coffee-brown, hairless.

'Excuse me.'

She had found the book she was looking for. She plucked it from the shelf with her thumb and second finger.

'Sandra.' It was Sally. 'I meant to ask you. How is your brother?'

'Better. Much better.'

'Please,' he said.

But she was moving toward the check-out, brushing a carpet-wrinkle from her kneecaps.

'Please,' he said. 'Acknowledge me.'

Professor Lunders had nearly finished. The board was covered. Now he was ballooning the lists of names and dates, drawing lines between them with white chalk, arrows with yellow chalk, and serrated lines with purple chalk that did not show up so well because the day was bright, and the blind-cord had snapped.

'So you see,' he said.

The class made notes, some lazily, others closely. All the chairs in the room were for right-handed people. She had her notebook on her lap, and was bent over it. He could count every vertebra, down to the seventh. She was wearing a mauve halter-neck blouse, although mauve was not her colour. It dipped almost to her coccyx. Why had he not noticed before that she was left-handed? He had been watching her for two and a half weeks. Was he so unobservant? Or was her presence such that a man failed to notice the obvious? Wasn't this what Keats had said somewhere? He would look it up.

'So you see,' Professor Lunders said, blowing chalk-dust from the edges of his nails. 'Heraclitus opts for motion. Everything is on a giddy, pellmell, dissociative rampage. Surface appearances alone indicate this. Turbulence is the proper condition in which we subsist. Our perceptual skills have to acknowledge the provisional nature of their conclusions insofar as the material underpinning those conclusions is inherently unstable. In other words, we can't see straight. Everything is in flux. What can we bring to bear on it? How can we anchor ourselves in it?'

Her arms. Where they bent at the elbow. When she straightened her arm, and ran her hand along its length, he could see that the crook of the elbow was moist. The underside of her arm was very pale, with one blue vein in the centre.

'For our next meeting, you might think about these things. You might ask yourselves whether it's possible to extrapolate a moral dimension from Heraclitus. Does his physics propose an ethics? And if so, how would that ethics utter itself?'

There was something else. A week before, he had noticed fine, dark hairs on her upper lip. In half-light, they were definite. In the light of the library, he had seen them, been stirred by them. Now they were gone. Had she shaved them? Did she not know that they would grow back twice as fast? He leaned closer, tightening his eyelids.

They were there still. Only whitened. Or bleached. Little, blonde hairs downing her lip. How soft they must be.

'Ciao,' said Professor Lunders to the class.

*

Yet it was at night when he couldn't see her quite so clearly, when she bent into the light of her desk-lamp on the third floor of the Green Library, her feet wound around each other, her espadrilles kicked off, that he liked best to study her. At the beginning, she had worn her hair down, or in a single plait. But during the second week of term the first bat of the hot fall found its way through an open window. For a while, no one noticed it. Then short shrieks from terrorized women brought the library assistants rushing with a polythene sack. The bat shot straight along the avenues of shelves. Frantic, it spun and dodged until, worn out, it dropped in a brown heap in the Jewish studies section.

After that, most of the women who read on the third floor wore hats, caps, hair-nets, and one, absurdly, a balaclava. There was a rumour that the little creatures couldn't free themselves from human hair. He missed the fall of her hair at night, the way she held it to one side with her free hand; but the other arrangement, her hair gathered into a bun at the top of her head, had its merits too: her face became still sharper, more severely classical; and her neck, bare and brown, seemed offered.

Acknowledge me, he thought. Please.

Yet he gave it up in time. This woman was absorbed. There was a pool of light at her own desk where she worked; around it, in the half-lit, slippered library, the silence and the shadow may have included other people, or they may not have. He had left the Zen book on his own desk one night. She always passed there; and she might notice it, might even have put a search for it at the library counter. But she had walked past in a taffeta shirt, head slanted, the picture of middle distances.

Three evenings before, who had arrived to speak with her but Sally Donovan.

'How've you been, Sally?'

'Fine.'

'What's in the brown bag?'

'Eucalyptus pods. I pick them whenever I have a free hand.'

'I just love the smell of eucalyptus pods,' said Sandra Solomons.

'You want some? I have plenty. They make your drawer smell so fresh. They keep your clothes so fresh.'

'I know. I just love to put them in my drawer.'

In the end, she got a half-dozen. While she was working, she arranged them in a line along the edge of the desk. Later, the movement of paper jogged one off the table on to the carpet. When she left, she had either forgotten her count, or she had other things in her mind.

It was a start. He picked it up on the way out, and put it in his pocket. Now he had that, a piece of paper on which she had written 'The Search for Perminence in a World . . .', before crumpling it up and tossing it into the waste-bin, and a pen. There had also been a spoiled Kleenex tissue and a Hershey chocolate wrapping-paper, but to have kept those would have been odd. There was a limit to what you could keep. In the absence of theatre tickets or strands of hair, crumpled essay titles and writing pens had to make do. But they were not ideal.

On the way home, he went on revolving the eucalyptus button between his fingers. All night, his palps kept its sweet, late-evening smell.

The day before, they had been in the Language Laboratory. He was studying French; when he took off his headphones, he realized that she was practising her Italian. She was two cubicles up and one in. They were alone.

'La famiglia ha tre bambini,' he heard her say.

'Please acknowledge me,' he said, holding his headphones in his hands.

'Io desidero parlare la lingua Italiana,' she said to the front of the cubicle.

'I have watched you for three weeks,' he said to her. 'For three weeks have I watched you.'

'Che volete?'

'I desire you. I desire you always to ignore me. I desire you always to be unapproachable, to be beyond me, to give me a purpose, to sweeten my life with failure. I desire you not to desire me, and so to heighten my desire for you.'

'Io voglio, egli –.'

'I would give anything,' he said. 'No sacrifice would be too great. I would become hollow for you. I would give you my kidney. I would give you my cornea. I would give you my bone-marrow.'

'Che bella. Tutto va bene.'

She opened her mouth very wide, and extended her lips, as if she were showing her teeth, or sucking.

When she leaned a little forward, he saw that she was not wearing any headphones.

Tonight he would know. Perhaps he had been mistaken. Perhaps he was terribly deceived. One thing only he was quite sure of: no woman had ever entered him in this way before. No woman had been so present to him, so elusive of him. But he would let her speak first. He had made himself plain to her. He could do no more.

At eight sharp, she arrived. Her hair was made up severely. She was wearing a white sun-suit, flip-flop sandals, a bright yellow lambswool cardigan for later when she would have to go home in the cold and darkness. At eight-five, she was lost to him. Her features diminished as the light failed.

He had been wrong again. Perhaps she had only removed the headpiece as she finished her lesson. She was oblivious of him. He watched her closely for a few minutes as she wrote quickly and noiselessly in her jotter. What could she be reading from?

'Flux,' he read as he turned to the first of his students' essays, 'is very important in the system of Heraclitus.'

The black ball of her hair was a still point. This was all he had a right to ask of her.

After a while, she got tired. She pressed her eyes with her thumbs. Perhaps she was vain, and needed glasses. Vanity went with coldness. Or perhaps she had been working too hard. That would be an opportunity for saying something. It could hardly seem pushy if he offered her a coffee.

'You look as tired as I do. Fancy a bad coffee from the vending-machine?'

But he could not endure the possibility of refusal.

Now she was stretching out for a sleep, folding her arms beneath her and resting her head on them, with her face turned away. She had done that before, but not for weeks. Even as ever, the light from the desk-lamp bore down on her bent neck. He was very happy. Nobody else was reading in that area. He alone had her secret. He was a party to her sleeping.

Time passed. Small noises from the lower floors of the library came weakly to the Archaeology section in which one wakeful, one sleeping student, kept a kind of acknowledged company. Once, twice maybe, there was the short suction sound of the elevator going up or going down. Later, a trolley squeaked on the far carpeting. A cough: deliberately, to clear the throat. Giggles in the stairwell. A brief flip-flopping, picking up speed: a girl running to an elevator as the doors started closing.

She was sleeping deeply. She was all out. It made him tired to look at her.

When the bat clumped against the slant windows above him, he thought she would wake. If she didn't, it would be a perfect occasion for him to rouse her. On the other hand, woken persons felt hostile toward those who shook them from their inside world. So he let it make a rush at the black windows, let it waver and fall almost casually toward the shelves, then pick itself up off the carpet to bound toward the stairwell and the illuminated library maps.

She never stirred. Down below, he could hear a muffled commotion: some voices, scampering footsteps, a laugh, a cry, more artificial than felt. It was as well she was dead to it all. Women scared easily. How many of them would stop to think that the bat was as terrified, as blinded, as confused and overcome, as any of them?

Pretty soon, the noises stopped. Minutes later, the library assistant came on to the public address system.

'The panic is over, guys,' said the librarian. 'This latest sneak attack by the enemy has been routed. Go back to your football magazines.'

She was still in another world.

At midnight, she always left. The last University bus round the campus was at twelve-fifteen. He thought to wake her, but decided not to. The library didn't close; there was a coffee-machine, a chocolate machine, a sandwich machine which was mostly out, and a machine that sold toothbrushes to persons who wanted to freshen up. The most that could happen would be if she woke feeling stiff. Sleeping in a sitting position did strange things to the circulation; but the soreness wore off soon.

When the automatic windows closed to prevent other bats

from disturbing the students of Stanford, and quick clickety sounds travelled up and down the length of the heating system, he was sure she must wake. But she slept it through. Moonlight glittered on the non-glare windows near her desk, and glittered on the cone of the desk-lamp, on the catch of the shapeless purse beside her elbow, on the bone pin in the bun of her piled hair.

It is your strangeness that keeps me here, he thought.

Finally, he went over to her, but softly. He kneeled beside her, leaned forward, listened. Then touched her. She was cold as moon. A little wet came from her mouth: neither warmth, nor breath, nor the smell of sleep on it.

'When I saw you for the first time,' he said, 'I went back to the seat you had been working at, and I touched the seat-cover. It was still warm. For two days, I was guilty.'

He placed her espadrilles neatly beside her.

'I saw you again in the library,' he said to the dead girl. 'You were alone at the photocopier. You were making copies. I hoped you would run out of dimes, and ask me if I had any. I had gone to the counter, and got a dollar's worth. But you had more in your backpack in one of those dime-holders that the banks give out. The photocopier kept working. There were flashes of light. The light travelled up and down your face, making your eyes shine and then water, making your teeth glint.'

Each of the three pens he capped, and laid them out side by side.

'Outside the coffee-house, I lost my appetite, watching you. I wanted so much to speak with you. Jays picked at the peas on my plate as I sat without eating.'

He tidied the books on the desk, putting them one on another, the soft-covered over the hardback, all the spines facing the one way.

Moonlight glittered like knives and forks, like a tray of cutlery spilled at her feet.

'I followed you to the Lake,' he said. 'I loved the little bit of grey sand that stuck to your instep, and the bottom of your bikini when you stood up.' He bundled her papers together, the green pad on the white one.

'Do you remember Professor Lunders' last lecture?' he said to her. 'When you stood up at the end, I could not help watching the static cling on your taffeta skirt. It shrank against your thighs so beautifully. I think Professor Lunders may have noticed it too. That was why I felt badly about his asking you to go have coffee with him.'

And he shut her bag, pressing down the contents in order to pull the zip to the very end of the track.

'It was me who finished your coffee that day in the coffee-house,' he said. 'When you came in from buying your packet of Winston, I could see how puzzled you were. I knew what you were thinking. For just one moment, I could see inside your mind. You were thinking: Did I finish my coffee, or just half of it?'

Her shoulders were very cold. He arranged the lambswool cardigan around them.

'But the best of all,' he said, 'and that is why I have kept it back, was when you stood in the fountain, and then sat down in it, on the way from the lecture because the sun was so hot. People stopped to look at you, to admire you. When you stood up, water just poured out of your clothes. A few people clapped. Two jumped in, and the three of you danced, there in the water, in green knee-deep water.'

Quickly, he picked out the bone pin, and loosened the two stretch-bands in her hair. The hair never budged, so he stirred it with his fingers until the pile began to work loose.

'The bat has gone,' he said to her. 'There is nothing to be afraid of.'

When the library was almost empty, and even the library assistants were looking very far away, he went out on to the terrace of the fourth-floor reading-room. Under the high frameless window, wet all over with moonlight, he could see the plants and shrubs blackening the embankments around the benches and the white, urn-like trash-cans. He could smell the plants too, their live stink almost solid in darkness.

He worked quickly. The librarians had a habit of stealing through the quieter sections in the small hours, to ensure that nothing unwholesome or undesirable in such a centre of research was occurring under cover of moonlight. Weeks before, the Basement Stacks had been closed at midnight after two young men had been surprised in the Primitive Greek Morality Section. Only two nights before, he had been woken by one, and asked if he wished to sleep or to study.

'I am sorry for leaving you alone for so long,' he said to her when he came in from the Smoking Terrace. 'I am going to stay with you now until the morning. The two of us together. It is the least I can do. In the last few weeks, I have sometimes felt a little bad about certain things. When I was about to keep the candy wrapper-paper, I began to wonder whether things were getting out of hand. At one or two moments, I seriously doubted the normality of my conduct. What you have done tonight dignifies my preoccupation with you. It elevates out of mere curiosity and randomness a desire that would otherwise strike the censorious as kinky. Now I can understand why I stopped, and followed you with my eyes, that first night at the check-out downstairs.'

He laid them at her feet, clumps and cuttings. The plants he had worked easily from the soil, the shrubs he had had to tug harshly, and to saw through with the corners of his housekeys. At her feet, he laid them, and piled them in layers. In the morning, their colours would blaze into being: the red hot cat's tail and the kaffir lily, the bat wings and the zebra plant, the crown of thorns and the weeping fig.

Moonlight glinted through the high, smoked windows. His hands were scratched and wet, damp under the nails. He kneeled down beside her, and rested his head on her lap. Outside, it was still black. He would have to be gone before it got too bright. But that was hours away. Meantime, she needed him. It was so lonely leaving your body, and going out without any clothes into great darkness. You got so used to being inside, to being warm. She would be looking back every so often to see if anyone were still standing at the door, in the square of light, with an arm raised. It would only be natural.

'You mustn't be frightened,' he said to her, and cried a little. 'I won't go away.'

INCIDENT ON THE EL CAMINO REAL

JOSEPH SAW the woman from about two hundred yards. She had her thumb out and she was moving it quite lazily as if she had been there a long time. But it was still early morning, and people going to work had other things on their minds. The best time for hitching was in the evening when the home-bound traffic was inching along slowly, and the people driving out of the city were starting to feel lonely and frightened again as they made their way back to their wives and children. Then it was nice to have company: college kids only had to look semi-normal to get a ride, and if a good-looking one just wiggled her butt a bit, she could cause a pile-up. At the start of the day, it was different: you were either bone-weary from the night before, or you were bent on making that day, that particular day, the one that would mark the change, the one that would bring about the difference, the one that would for ever divide the days of your life into those that came before and those that followed after. The last thing you wanted was to volley pleasantries with a perfect stranger as you shot on course and on target down the arrow-straight stretches of the Camino Real.

As it happened, Joseph had climbed between the sheets at a reasonable hour the night before; and he had long since given up on the early morning buzz. One day was much like another, and he liked it that way. He had been through the guess-what-tomorrow-might-bring phase, but that was sophomore territory. He was into a futility syndrome now. Life was a pain in the ass. You minimized the pain and you maximized the ass; that way, Tuesday passed into Wednesday, Wednesday into Thursday, with little comment and less crisis. Weekends, you partied. Also, Joseph had people in his life: he loved the woman he was living with, and he kind of liked her child too. He had never known what it was to have a kid brother. Now he could talk to Benjamin, and tell him stories about the Bible and space-wars, and promise to take him to Disneyland some day, and teach him the difference between coniferous and deciduous, and about whales, and Marconi, and why capital punishment is wrong.

'But why is it wrong?' Benjamin would say.

'Because,' Joseph would tell him. 'Anyhow, how would you like to have your head chopped off?'

'But they don't do that now. What they do is they fry you in the chair, or they inject you.'

'That's worse,' Joseph said. 'That's a perversion of medical progress.'

And they would go on and on.

Joseph checked the time. He had an hour before that Freshman Composition class. All he had to do was be there on time. No students were coming to see him, their papers were graded, he had the handouts done already. There might even be time to let a coffee get cold while he read the *Chronicle* in the University coffee-house. He liked that slow-start approach to the day. So he swung over to the kerb, and pulled up. The woman ran the few feet to the car. Joseph only had seconds to realize that his first impressions had been overly negative: she was more than average, she was nice. Twenty-five, twenty-seven, good teeth, blondish, biggish boobs, cord trousers, boots. As she ducked her face down to the window, she held her hair back with her hand. He could see the slim tan-mark of a wrist-watch.

'Where to?' Joseph said.

'That depends,' said the woman, getting in.

Even before he had reached across her to close the door, the scent of whatever she was wearing filled the car.

To begin with, they talked shop.

'Do you go to school?' she said to Joseph.

'I used to go to school,' he said. 'Now I teach. I teach at a Jesuit place.'

'You're not a priest, are you?'

'No,' Joseph said. 'My father was a wealthy Jew from New York. He was a very lugubrious man.'

'Are you a wealthy Jew?' she asked.

'My finances are so-so,' he said. 'I am not neurotic about them.'

She was quiet for a few minutes. Joseph thought she might be nervous. She was holding her cotton handbag tightly, and staring out the window as if she had never seen such interesting store-fronts. Yet she was tapping her foot to the music on the radio. If she was agitated, she would hardly keep time to a pop song, let alone a pop song that was so mediocre. Joseph switched to another band, to a news update. Her foot kept tapping.

'Are you all right?' he said to her.

'Uh huh.'

She didn't have a gun in the bag, did she? Was she crazy? If it was a heist, she would surely team up with some other guy. She couldn't pull it off all by herself. Maybe she was just a bit odd, a bit uptight. Maybe she thought he was bizarre because he had used the word 'lugubrious'. Or perhaps she had personal problems. She hadn't just come from anywhere. She had come out of a situation, a background, a context.

'Lugubrious means kind of woeful, very down,' Joseph said.

She had made up her mind about something. She turned to look at him.

'Ever feel very horny in the morning?' she said to him. 'I mean, first thing in the morning, do you ever feel like pussy?'

'Don't talk like that,' Joseph said.

She was taken aback, baffled even.

'You mind me talking about sex?'

'The topic is fine with me,' said Joseph. 'I guess I'm a romantic about it. I don't much like dirty language. "Horny", and "pussy", and that stuff.'

The woman might not have anticipated this contingency, but she adapted to it, and coped with it. That was because she was flexible.

'When you wake up,' she said to him, 'and you're on your own, do you ever want to be with a woman, to share what you have to give with a woman, to have a relationship with her?'

'Why do you ask?'

'Because I could make you very happy for a few minutes, if you wished it. I could bring something special into your drive to work. I mean, it wouldn't delay your getting there on time. You wouldn't have to pull in, or go somewhere. You could just keep driving.'

Joseph looked at her critically. She seemed to be for real. She spoke nicely, her skin was clear, she dressed neatly, almost stylishly, and she smelled like a perfume counter. But what did that tell you? You could be beautiful, and still psychotic. Look at Catherine the Great, who copulated with stallions. Or you could be handsome, a fine-looking man, and be deranged. Look at the Joint Chiefs of Staff. There was one who might have been Rembrandt with less hair, and who liked nothing better than to throw out a strike-first line at Commencement Days. Colour schemes and well-shaped fingernails proved nothing. Inside a person's head was a mystery, a closed book.

'Are you a Fairy Godmother?' Joseph asked her. 'Or a professional?'

'I'm just an ordinary girl,' she said. 'This is a whole new thing for me.'

'Are you attracted to me? Is it my aftershave, or my mouthwash, or maybe the fact that I drive a European car?'

'Questions, questions,' she said. 'I can give you a handjob for twenty-five bucks. But please stop asking me questions.'

'I hate that word too. I hate that word "handjob".'

'I can satisfy your manhood. I can release the passion in your loins.'

'I prefer that,' he said. 'I like appropriate diction. It confers dignity on things.'

'Twenty dollars is not much. You would pay more for a parking violation. But thirty is thirty. So I thought twenty-five.'

'Twenty-five is all right,' Joseph said. He was beginning to feel comfortable with the situation. It was not everyday, of course, but it was not extraordinary either. What made it seem unusual was the hour of the day. It was still early. The guy in the next lane was shaving, one hand on the wheel, his neck arched high while he ran the battery razor up and down the sides of his Adam's apple. That was what made for the sense of unreality. If it was dark, you would not give it a second thought. After all, he had been relieved of his tensions in automobiles on maybe a half-dozen occasions. The cars had all been stationary at the time, it was true. Still, Joseph was a safe driver. In fact, he had the lowest premium of any thirty-year-old he knew. Anyhow, even with the risk, it would be a hell of a story.

'How are we off for time?' said the woman.

'We're fine for time,' he said. And he waited to see what she would do next. It crossed his mind that she might be a police officer, but it seemed unlikely. After all, the courts had ruled against that kind of harassment, and this was not New York. This was the Camino Real, the distance between A and B, the forty minutes of easy music and a sluggish stick shift between home, where the garden sprinklers made a sound like coffee-vending machines, and work, where the coffee-vending machines made a noise like garden sprinklers. This was not hallowed ground: it was safe ground. So Joseph waited. He could afford to.

At first, she rummaged in her handbag, taking out compacts and atomisers. Finally she found the packet she was looking for.

'I can't wear condoms,' Joseph said. 'They dishearten me. Anyhow, I live a perfectly above-suspicion, clean-living kind of life. Sometimes I think that I may marry the woman I am sharing everything with right now, and that would prove my altruism, because I have had quite a few not-nice-at-all experiences with ladies.'

The woman went through her bag again, and came up with a double-fold cotton diaper. Perhaps she had a baby, or perhaps she diapered clients. After all, the most colourful oddballs flourished along the Camino Real, not to mention the City. Joseph just wished that the woman would put away those awful prophylactics.

'Careful now,' he said to her as she tugged at his zip. 'Mind my hairs.'

'It's a very strong zip,' she said. 'Can you lift up off the seat a bit, so I can get your trousers down?'

Joseph tried this, but it was difficult. His foot sank a little hard against the pedal, and the car surged forward. The chap who was shaving looked annoyed; then his own car picked up speed, drew level, pulled ahead.

'This is ridiculous,' Joseph said. 'I can't drive with my trousers round my knees. I'll do it.'

He got his zip down, but he couldn't pull his briefs aside to free his penis. Why did he wear such tight underwear? Apart all together from that talk about cancer of the testis, it let you down so badly at moments like these. No wonder he was beginning to feel vulnerable.

'I know how,' said the woman, and she did too. Joseph winced a little as she worked him loose. While still an adolescent, he had had a traumatic encounter with a zip fastener. These things went deep.

'There now,' said the woman. 'Where have you been hiding?'

Joseph switched lanes. There was a Santrams bus coming in fast behind him; he could do without a burst of bluecollar applause. All those people on buses ever did was look into cars in a bored, accusing manner. It would put anybody off.

'What do you call him?' the woman said.

'What do you mean "Call him"?'

'It, then. Most men have a name for it. Their own name.'

Certain things are sacred. Joseph was not about to make free with something as intimate as a name. Even the woman he lived with called him by his special word rarely.

'I'm not most men,' Joseph said. He said it nearly as well as Joseph Cotten had said it the night before, on that film he could not remember the title of. In fact, he thought he gave it an extra something, a frisson.

But the woman spread the diaper out on his lap, and touched him here and there, deftly.

'You can tell me,' she said.

'Excalibur,' he said.

'He looks his name,' she said. 'If I had to think of a name, that is the one I would think of.'

'It is from the Arthurian cycle,' said Joseph. 'From the King Arthur legends. It has nothing to do with guns.'

Already, in his heart of hearts, he was sorry he had told her. But it was too late now. Besides, there was a good chance she would forget. It was a long word. So Joseph closed his eyes as often as he could, when the road ahead was clear, and he thought about the second girl in the Dairy Produce advertisement that he had seen five times, spanking the dark girl with the little mole on her throat, who hardly ever said anything in class and always asked for an extension on her assignments.

The woman beside him kept on talking.

'Have you something you want to give me, Excalibur?' she said. 'I have the strangest feeling you want to give me something.'

Joseph checked his rear-view mirror. The bus was way behind him. Then he shut his eyes again. This time, he reversed the spanking scenario. Now he had the girl with the mole smacking the woman in the milk commercial. Actually, that was much nicer.

'What's happening?' he heard her say. 'What's happening?'

Joseph was feeling generous as he backed into his space in the faculty parking area.

'Would you like a cup of coffee?' he said to the woman. She had been quiet for a time, glancing out the side-window, her thumbs flicking open and snapping shut the catch of her handbag. It was strange how she moved from reserve to the other. She was a complete mystery to him. If he had met her at a function, he would probably have been attracted to her. At none of the parties he attended would she have seemed in any way out of place, a rank outsider. She would have fitted in more easily than some of his own colleagues, especially the guys from the Art Department, or the women in Linguistics.

'That would be nice,' she said.

Joseph wondered about the money. He suspected she would want it now. Over coffee and bagels it would be inappropriate to count out dollar bills. It might even draw attention to them. Better to pay her, and have done with it. Still, he waited. He hoped she might ask him for the twenty-five bucks. That would signal the close of business, the end of the contract. He would prefer her to say it, because that would identify her more clearly. As it was, she was beginning to seem remote, complex even. She had a faraway, very alert expression, which bothered him. It would be nicer if she was nonchalant, and bantered with him.

'What's your name?' she said to him.

'Jon,' he said. 'My parents say Jonathan, my friends say Jonnie.'

'Jonathan is nice,' she said.

'I can live without it,' Joseph said. 'I like Jon better.'

He liked the woman well enough, but you had to be careful. Names were dynamite. Joseph was still a little unhappy that he had given away Excalibur. It was true that women could worm anything out of you. The Samson story said it all. Malory was full of it too.

'My name is Elinor,' said the woman.

Joseph thought that was most unlikely.

'I knew two Elinors, back east,' he said. 'Elinor is a neat name.'

They said nothing for a few minutes. Joseph could hear the hood ticking as it cooled, and the woman breathing through her nose. She had a slight sinus problem.

'Were they like me?' she said finally.

'More or less,' Joseph said.

Joseph's mistake was to offer her food as well. Still, it was typical of him: he was basically good-natured. She chose a portion of taramasalata in a ramekin dish, and some ripe Dolcelatte from the cheeseboard. These things were not inexpensive. He was tempted to take it out of her twenty-five. The taramasalata on its own was four dollars, almost twice the cost of the vegetable rissole he had pointed out to her.

'If you want to eat the taramasalata out of the ramekin, you have to pay ten dollars indemnity,' the assistant at the check-out said to Elinor. Joseph made her go back, and scoop the salad into a styrofoam bowl.

'There is a notice to that effect,' said the assistant.

'I know,' Joseph said. 'It's been a strange morning.'

The woman who called herself Elinor reappeared at his side. Joseph checked his watch against the clock over the check-out. He had fifteen minutes.

'Ramekin is a nice word,' the woman said. 'That's two new words inside an hour.'

It vexed him that she was still holding on to that private pet-name. As an endearment, it would be finito if she uttered it again.

'Yes?' he said.

'Ramekin,' she said. 'And before that, lugubrious.'

That was the topic he settled on, to steer him over the fifteen minutes. Words, and what happens to them. Actually, it was Joseph's territory. Besides, it was a warm-up exercise, a workout before class. He was going to talk about meaning, and then hand back their assignments. He might as well start now.

'You were saying you liked "lugubrious",' he said.

She talked through the taramasalata.

'Me, I love words too,' Joseph said. 'I look around, and I

see the saddest things happening to them. Once you created
the cosmos, now you create a hairstyle. To speculate was to
think, to wonder, to live the life of the mind, to mind the life
of the mind.'

Joseph thought that was rather good.

'Uh huh,' she said, through the taramasalata.

'Now it's to buy real estate, or to fool around with venture
capital. The same thing happened to "rationalize". I mean,
just look at it. To reason, to order the world in a scientific
manner. Now they use it to lay off people.'

'It's terrible,' she said.

'I hate to see language being prostituted,' Joseph said.

As he said this, a young girl approached the table. She
would have to be the dark one with the little mole on her
throat; and she was.

'Joseph,' she said. 'I wanted to catch you before class. I
need an extension.'

'We'll talk later,' he said.

When she moved on, the woman who called herself Elinor
looked at him. She had really demolished that taramasalata.

'Joseph?' she said.

'I am Joseph here,' he said. 'In my other job, I am Jon. I
moonlight. My tax is very convoluted. Joseph is my second
name.'

'That's strange,' she said. 'My second name is Elinor. We
seem to like second names, the two of us. We share a lot.'

'You want us to be on first-name terms?' said Joseph.

'No,' she said. 'I've known you as Jon for so long, I
couldn't begin to think of you as Joe. Joey perhaps, or Little
Joe. Maybe even Jo-Jo.'

Joseph was at a loss what to say. Even if she was not a
hooker, she could hardly have a sense of irony. People with a
sense of irony did not go around the place, relieving other

people of their tensions. More likely she was being nice, and grateful for the taramasalata. When you thought about it, she could only be dull average at best.

'I must go now,' he said. He opened his wallet, and counted out thirty dollars in six five-dollar bills. Back home, he could say it had been stolen.

'You're a nice person,' he said. 'The extra five is to say that.'

'You go,' she said. 'I have to finish my cheese.'

'Couldn't you take it with you?'

'I want to wash up after my cheese,' she said. 'I can't hitch a ride back to where you picked me up, smelling of cheese and salad.'

That floored him. The idea had never entered his head. Obviously, he was not dumbfounded. Nowadays, people tend not to be. Surprise is very uncommon. Still, he was taken aback. If necessary, the class could wait a few minutes.

'Are you going to go through this whole routine again?' he said.

'What did you think? Did you think I was going to ride a bus?'

'But how can you do that? How can you do it again? A second time?'

'Third,' she said.

'I find this revolting. I am not highly strung, but I find this too much.'

'You know any other way to raise four hundred dollars by six o'clock tonight?'

'You need four hundred dollars by six?'

'I need three hundred twenty dollars,' she said.

Joseph had not forgotten his simple arithmetic.

'You got fifty dollars from some guy?'

'I got fifty dollars from a guy with a button-down shirt and a pearl necktie pin.'

[180]

Simple arithmetic did not, however, extend into fractions.

'How often can you do this in a day?' Joseph asked her.

'As often as I meet people like you,' she said. 'Are there many people like you?'

'After I buy you breakfast, you ridicule me,' he said. 'After I buy you taramasalata at four dollars.'

He could not endure her now. He stood up and strode off. The whole affair had been a mistake: picking her up, telling about Excalibur, the line about Jon, the salad and cheese, the extra five bucks. He had been born yesterday. He would never learn sense. If you were kind, if you opened up to other people, they would only manipulate and exploit you. Then they would add insult to injury by abusing you to your face. He should have thrown her out of the car as soon as she had said 'That depends'. To think that she had just climbed out of another car. That was the most sordid part.

At the swing-door of the coffee house, he looked back briefly. She was sitting over her Dolcelatte, holding her head with both hands as if it had broken off and she was waiting, trying not to move, until the glue hardened.

All the way home in the car, Joseph thought about her. What kind of a person could spend her day driving up and down the Camino Real, performing sexual acts with complete strangers? She must have been very crazy. She may even have been psychotic. If he read in the morning paper about some poor guy who had been stabbed a billion times, he would know where to point the finger. It was only a matter of time before she showed herself in her true colours. The way she disguised herself was effective, but she could not keep it up forever. Neat clothes and clear skin might deceive for a time; sooner or later, her fidgeting would give her away. He could properly be thankful that she had not been violent in the car.

Even allowing for his superior strength as a male, she might have caused a pile-up in the few seconds of confused tussling while he sought to restrain her. These were not pleasant thoughts, but they had to be faced.

Joseph stopped at the only florist's which was still open.

'Something really nice,' he said to the man in the store. 'Up to thirty dollars.'

'For thirty dollars,' the man said, 'we can do something very special.'

There was another possibility. It too had to be confronted. She might attempt to blackmail him. She knew his first name, she knew where he worked, she had probably made a note of the car registration. If she wanted to, she could find out where he lived.

'These are not honeysuckle,' the man said, 'but you would have to be in the business to tell the difference.'

She could not have spread infection. She had only touched him with her hands, not with her mouth. But what if the other guy had been dirty, and had left some germs on her fingers or under her nails? How long could germs live in the light? These days, you heard the most horrific stories about diseases. To listen to them would put you off your food. When he got home, he would wash in very hot water. If necessary, he would almost scald himself. Somewhere in the house was a new bottle of hydrogen peroxide.

'Put in more of the blue ones,' he said to the florist.

One explanation covered everything. She was a drug addict. How else could you explain her having to make up four hundred dollars by six o'clock? True, she didn't look like a junkie, but things were so deceptive in this world. She might be as full of puncture marks as a pin-cushion. He hadn't seen very much of her, and she was hardly going to shoot herself in the face or hands. Four hundred bucks would probably supply the fix she needed.

'More of the pink too,' Joseph decided.

'You don't want your colours to clash,' said the florist. 'You want them to co-operate.'

Finally, it was done. It was a lovely arrangement.

'Whoever the significant other in your life may be,' the man said, 'he or she is going to love this.'

'She deserves them,' Joseph said, accenting the pronoun.

'A woman in a thousand,' the florist said.

'A woman in a thousand,' Joseph agreed.

When Joseph got home again, it was already dark. He parked in the car-port and sat a while at the wheel, feeling the wet from the flower arrangement soak into his trouser-leg. He wished he had stayed in bed that morning. He wished he had woken with a strep throat or a sore tooth, and turned away from the window back into the warm duvet. And he wished he had washed his mouth or maybe eaten a Granny Smith and then made love to the woman he was living with, after Benjamin had gone out the pantry door to start his paper round. Because he was feeling strange now, like the way he did when he read the Psalms or the small side-columns in the Sunday papers about river blindness in African infants. He was feeling lost and found; he was feeling sad and singular; he was feeling shit.

He walked across the drive under starlight. Snails were mating on the tarmacadam under the porch-front canopy. Joseph picked his route delicately among their soapy huddles, but he couldn't avoid standing on one, and then of course he had to mash it into the pavement with the heel of his boot to make quite certain it was really dead and not left suffering. He had a conscience about these things, and about the eco-system too. He was not all bad.

Inside the house, Benjamin was watching the television. He was in the lotus position, and didn't look round. Only when Joseph plonked his briefcase on the loose floorboard and made the picture snow, did the boy turn toward him.

'They bar-be-cued that black guy in Miami this morning,' Benjamin announced. 'You know, the one that made the woman eat the parish letter.'

Joseph was not listening. When had he last brought her flowers, and would she suspect him for doing so? He had heard about that happening to a guy in Modern Languages. He had arrived home with fresh flowers, and his wife had only said: 'So, who's the competition?' She had been right too, but that was not the point. The point was that the woman he lived with had not been given flowers since the time she had terrible PMT, and threw the television out the bedroom window. Mind you, it was only a portable. And that was at least six months ago.

Anyhow, he gave them to her. She was in the kitchen, steeping a mohair cardigan. Her hands were red from the hairs, but that always happened. It was no use getting uptight about it. At least she liked the arrangement.

'Are these from Excalibur?' she asked him softly.

'Sort of,' Joseph told her. Why did she have to go and bring up Excalibur? There was no need.

The woman he was living with put her arms around him.

'I'll sit on your face tonight,' she said. 'As a special treat.'

Joseph tried to smile the way he was supposed to. It was difficult.

'I'll be back in a second,' he said. 'A call of nature.'

He went into the bedroom and lay on the bed. Then he got up and opened the mirrored doors of the double wardrobe. He opened them as wide as they would go, and held them back with shoes and a hatbox. He needed to lie down, but he could not bear to look at his own face while he did so.

THE FIGURE ON THE CROSS

Freddie always liked the church. It wasn't the least bit fashionable, of course, because it was dark and damp, with very inferior stained-glass windows, and wooden benches so tightly packed together that you chafed your ankles against the edge of the kneeler when you stood for the Gospel or to let someone pass. And the whole place smelled to high heaven of beeswax and chilly marble, brass plaques and the stiff, cool scent of altar cloth. When you spoke, your voice went skittering up the walls until it got well and truly lost in the great webbed ceiling; and when you walked, your steps snapped like a whiplash among all the statues that threw their eyes to Heaven, as much to say: is there any peace and quiet in this world?

Freddie went to the church to get away from everything. That's one of their uses, anyway, though they do have many others, including the opposite. The part of the place that he liked best was in one of the transepts where a splendid life-size statue of the crucified Christ hung from an oaken cross. There was a noisy heater there, and a rake of little candles weeping their eyes out as they spattered yellow light like bits and pieces of surgical dressing on the mangled feet of the figure on the crucifix. If you know that part of the world and the church I'm speaking of, you'll know Freddie as well, because he was the fellow with ginger hair who used to be there on each and every weekday afternoon when school ended. And why he was there only God knows.

Fr Leo, of course, was hell-bent on finding a reason.

'What in the name of God is that chap doing in here again? You'd need eyes in the back of your head to keep up with him.'

Fr Phil took a different attitude.

'Sure that's only Freddie from down the road. He wouldn't drown a wasp. I've known him since he fell out of the tree and had his arm in plaster for two months.'

'Listen to me, Fr Phil. I'm longer at this game than you are, and I know devilment like the back of my hand. No boy ever graced the inside of a church of his own free will. It was devilment brought that boy here. That's the God's truth, and well you know it.'

'He's a harmless lad, and he hasn't much home-life. He comes here for the peace and quiet.'

'I'll tell you this for nothing,' said Fr Leo. 'I'll give him peace and quiet if he so much as blinks.'

Now I don't have to tell you who those gentlemen were. The nasty one was the parish priest and the nice one was his curate. The parish priest had been cranky ever since the Second World War because that event confused him; and the young curate had been over the moon long before the first astronauts landed there, because he was quite convinced that the planet Earth is out of this world. Whenever he got excited, his spectacles would steam over and he'd trip on his own shoelaces. But the bad-tempered parish priest was a different matter entirely. If anything vexed him, the sweat-stains under his arms would grow and grow and grow until they met in the middle where his cassock was buttoned, and his nose would darken like a turnip. That was the way he went whenever he saw Freddie; but Freddie never noticed, because wise people notice very little. Instead, they practise at being quiet, the way Freddie was when he slipped into the church that Wednesday afternoon, sat down in his usual bench, scratched the tip of his nose, and said to the Figure on the Cross:

'Hello, Jesus.'

'Hello, Freddie.'

There was something of a pause at this point; and it was largely Freddie's.

'I . . . beg your pardon.'

'There's no need to,' said the Figure on the Cross. 'When I heard the rain turning to sleet, I thought to myself: He won't come today. He'll go home instead. Are you wet through?'

'No . . . sir,' Freddie said.

'Sit on the heater where it's cosy. But don't make a practice of it. I understand you can get piles that way.'

'Yes . . . sir.'

'The bells begin to ring at four,' said the Figure on the Cross. 'The stones of the church vibrate minutely, and the tremors journey through the wood of the cross. Then I know. I say to myself: Freddie will be here on the sixth bong; and you always are.'

'Am I?' Freddie said.

'Always. Except the time you fell out of the tree and ended up with your arm in plaster.'

'I remember.'

'I was lonely for weeks until you came again,' said the Figure on the Cross. 'Then I looked down on the sixth bong one day, and the nice curate was writing his name on the plaster-cast. And you were grinning up at me. Promise me you won't climb trees that high again. Especially not as a dare. Dares are for weaklings. When a bully dares you, you should tell him to shove it.'

'I . . . promise,' Freddie said.

'Thank you.'

A boy of only fourteen can hardly help being curious; and Freddie was curious about one thing in particular.

'You're . . . you're . . . well . . .'

'Yes?'

'You're not like the picture of you.'

'Which picture is that ?'

'The . . . one in my bedroom. Where you're pointing at your heart, and your eyes follow me everywhere, from the wardrobe to the window. And wherever I look at you, you're looking at me.'

'I know the one you mean,' said the Figure on the Cross. 'I was never very fond of it. I look too severe, don't I? It would make you nervous. But what could I say? The artist was one of my closest friends; and he meant well.'

'Are you . . . are you . . .'

'Yes.'

'Are you very sore on the cross?'

'A little. My hands and my feet are numb.'

'I'm sorry.'

'Thank you.'

'Shall I . . . shall I rub your feet for you, and make them warm?'

'That would be . . . wonderful.'

After that, Freddie made extra certain to be in the church at the foot of the cross on the sixth bong of the big bells. Mind you, once he tried to time it to perfection, he would always arrive a little early or a little late; but he never failed to come. He was a mystery to Fr Leo, because the parish priest couldn't decide what he was up to. After all, there wasn't any money to be stolen out of the collection boxes: only buttons off hassocks and Spanish pesetas from the package holidays the parishioners went on. So the priest was baffled.

'What the devil's going on?' he said to Fr Phil. 'Is he after the brass candlesticks? Or the fresh flowers off the altar?'

'God knows,' said Fr Phil. 'Would you not leave him be? Look, wasn't I playing conkers with him the other day in the church porch, and I asked him myself.'

'And what did he say?'

'He said if I didn't know, he couldn't tell me.'

'Oh, the rudeness! By God,' said Fr Leo, 'in my day a clip on the ear worked wonders. A clip on the ear was your only answer. I tell you this for nothing: things have gone downhill since the clip on the ear went out.'

'Is that better?' said Freddie. He had become something of an expert at warming feet. If he stood on the heater, he could just about reach one of the hands as well, but only enough to touch for a few, wobbly seconds.

'Much. You have very gentle hands.'

'My mother says I'm a butterfingers.'

'That's only because of her headaches.'

'And my dad says he has no time for religion.'

'The prophets were like that too,' said the Figure on the Cross.

'Because my dad says so many people have been killed in the name of God.'

'It happened to me.'

Freddie couldn't think of anything to say to that, so he breathed as warm as he could on the chilled feet of the figure.

'Have I upset you now?' he said finally.

'You could never do that, Freddie.'

Freddie was glad again; and when he was glad, he thought in a practical manner.

'Are you . . . are you hungry?'

'A little.'

'And thirsty?'

'Yes.'

'I have an orange drink, but the fizz has gone out of it. And I have two egg sandwiches from my lunch. They smell of tupperware a bit, but they're all right.'

'I'm sure they are.'

'I have a cup for the drink. Shall we share it?'

'Please.'

Freddie decided to take full advantage of this.

'And will you tell me more?' he said eagerly.

'Where was I when we stopped?' said the Figure on the Cross.

'We were still in Nazareth, and the dog was lost. But he came when you called.'

'That was because I didn't shout, you see. He was so tired he couldn't even wag his tail.'

'Why didn't you invent a helicopter and search for him that way?'

'There were no pilots in Palestine, Freddie. And besides, I'm not a magician. I'm a carpenter. I work in wood, and on it. People will never see the difference.'

Now all this time Fr Leo was still keeping both eyes on the little boy. He was so devilishly curious that, even if he was hearing Confession, he'd dart out now and again to make sure Freddie hadn't skedaddled with leaflets from the bookstand or vestments from the sacristy. In fact, the whole job of policing the precinct became something of an obsession with him. But he never caught Freddie at any kind of mischief, and this in itself annoyed him even more. All the boy ever seemed to do was sit giggling and wide-eyed at the foot of that ugly old crucifix that should have been chopped up for firewood years ago. But you couldn't turf him out just for that. So Fr Leo watched him more closely than ever with his strongest pair of glasses. Still he saw nothing; and that was because, in the sort of world we live in, only the blind can see straight.

Then one day a penny dropped in the man's mind.

'I've an idea,' he said to Fr Phil.

'You do?'

'I do indeed.'

'It isn't advisable,' said Fr Phil.

'I have it anyway,' said Fr Leo, 'and it's this: the boy is an imbecile. He's a simpleton, God love him.'

'I imagine God does love him,' Fr Phil said.

'That would make sense,' said Fr Leo. 'In fact, it would make perfect sense. It would explain everything.'

'You mean God loving him?'

'Are we on the same wavelength at all, Fr Phil? I mean his being simple.'

Fr Leo took off his glasses and examined the lenses as if he were inspecting his insights.

'Why the Devil did I never think of it before?' he said. 'Anyhow, I've solved the mystery.'

'Mysteries aren't made to be solved,' said Fr Phil. 'They are made to be minded.'

Freddie finally plucked up courage.

'You're very quiet today.'

'Am I?'

'Why . . . why were you . . .'

'Yes?'

'Why were you crying when I came in?'

There was a little silence.

'A friend of mine died a few moments ago in a large house all by himself in the middle of Mexico City. He was writing out a shopping list when it happened.'

'I'm sorry.'

'And a child in a suburb of Stockholm was struck for no reason so that her ear-drum burst and bled. Seconds before you arrived.'

'That was awful,' Freddie said.

'In a stony field on the island of Inishbofin, a fieldmouse is having her baby. Her tiny face is full of concentration. She can think of nothing else. And the planets circle her silently. They know their place.'

'Shall I . . . wipe your tears away?' said Freddie. 'I have a tissue that I only used a bit of.'

'Crying is good for you, Freddie.'

'Do you . . . cry often?'

'It depends.'

'When did you cry the most?'

'In a garden, a most beautiful garden full of rocks and rhododendrons. When I lifted my face to be kissed, and a man whom I loved very much stepped back and away as the soldiers swept round me. That was the hardest. My heart . . . broke like an eggshell.'

Freddie would have done anything that moment, but he could think of only one thing.

'Would it . . . would it help,' he asked, 'if I took out one of the nails? I could try to.'

'Would you?' said the Figure on the Cross.

Then Freddie got a firm grasp with both of his hands on the black spike that was driven deep into the ankles of the crucified Christ, and he pulled with all his might until he thought his heart would burst open; and then he pulled twice as hard, though the palms of his hands were aching as if he'd been beaten at school for missing a question – and slowly, slowly, slowly the nail began to loosen like the long root of a weed tugged inch by gradual inch out of the ground. From the bruised flesh of the instep he wrestled the rigid iron, though his own two hands were turning from pink to purple where the head of the nail was wedged between them. And then, just on the point of final exhaustion, the tautness and the tightness eased, the strain softened, and the nail slipped softly out. It fell with a heavy clunk on the marbled floor, and the tiny candles shivered as the sound passed through them.

Fr Leo came pounding toward the transept like the hammers of Hell.

'What in the name of God do you think you're up to?' he roared, shaking Freddie by the shoulders. 'You blasted hooligan! You corner-boy! You antichrist!'

And he gave the boy a good old-fashioned clip on the ear.

'I should boot you all the way from here to borstal. Now you take your schoolbag and your lunchbox, and you start running as hard as your heels will carry you, do you hear me? Because you don't eat egg sandwiches in the House of God, do you hear me? And you don't drink out of cans in a sacred place, do you hear me? And you don't dare touch, manhandle or otherwise interfere with any item of church property, do you hear me? Go smash up a bus-shelter for all I care; go walk your egg sandwiches into your living-room carpet for all I care; but if ever you darken this door again, I'll crucify you, do you hear me?'

Freddie heard very well. After all, the man was shouting so that he practically foamed at the mouth; and when he had done shouting, and given the boy an extra clip on the ear for good measure, Freddie gathered up his satchel and his lunchbox and his cellophane bag of marbles and rushed out of the church by the side-door only to discover that the afternoon had given up and that darkness was rubbing the sky like a stick of carbon. He had left behind him a little cutting from a local community newspaper about a swimming competition in which he had come second. He had wanted to read it to the Figure on the Cross, but he was too afraid to go back for it now.

A sharp, staccato burst of hammering filled the inside of the church. Fr Leo was working the nail back into its proper place.

'I can't get over the boy's strength,' said Fr Phil to Fr Leo.

'I tell you this,' he said to Fr Phil. 'I put the fear of God into him. He won't be back in a month of Sundays.'

'Sure he meant no harm at all,' Fr Phil said. 'It was only a notion that came into his head. You know the way kids imagine things.'

Fr Phil examined the face of the figure intently.

'It's strange,' he said. 'I never realized the thorns were real. I always assumed they were wooden, like the rest of it.'

But Fr Leo wasn't listening.

'It was devilment. Pure devilment. But I nailed him good and proper. There now. That'll hold. I'll just give it one good wallop, and we're home again.'

There was a final loud hammer-blow which made the candles tremble and the roses on the altar cringe.

'Done,' said Fr Leo with the satisfaction of a man who has reached his end. 'It would take a miracle to move that now.'

NAGASAKI

It is early in the morning of the ninth of August, 1945, and the clouds have parted over the city of Nagasaki to let the sun in. The horns and hooters of the distant shipyard are in full throat, a dawn chorus of screams and screeches that ricochet among the roof-slates of the houses by the harbour. They shriek so piercingly that Mrs Kawabata abandons her mangle and walks across her living-room to close the yellow shutters of her home in Natsue Street, while her husband, stone deaf since the death of their second son in Singapore three years ago, smiles at her amiably, and wipes his reading glasses with a piece of newsprint. He is deaf to the cries of this world, and has never looked younger.

On the other side of the city, where the sounds of the shipyard hooters die away, the noise of the coal tenders starts up. The length and breadth of the depot reverberate with the banging of engines, the incensed hiss of the iron wheels as they cool under the hoses, and the noise of the slow goods stopping with the sharp cry of pain that always reminds Mr Toraiwa of a dying pig as the knife sinks deeper. It reminds him of that now as he stands to remove his cap and fan his forehead. His face is flushed with the effort of loading coal, and a red wedge runs across his temples where the rim of the hat is too tight, and bites into the skin. But he can't rub his face with the back of his hand as he wants to, because they're both of them so dirty from hauling sacks that not even a pumice stone would ever make them clean. So he leans against the fender where the carriages are coupled, and he thinks of pigs strung tightly between the shafts of a cart, and he thinks of the farmyard where he grew up in the country near Nagoya. And that gives him the strength to resume the loading when the breeze has dried his neck.

But let's leave Mr Toraiwa to his memories and Mrs Kawabata to her mutterings. After all, they are only two persons out of how many who woke that morning of August the ninth to squint up at the sunlight, and wash their bodies in clear, cool water. Life had not singled them out in any strange or special way, and were it not that each had a daughter attending the German Convent near the Ministry of Finance, it is altogether likely that the only thing they would have had in common is the death they shared in a single instant. And to tell you that at the start is not to spoil the story. The story itself is thoroughly spoiled to begin with, and it has gone on to spoil everything else as well. For as Mr Toraiwa pulls his shirt collar this way and that to cool his throat, and as Mrs Kawabata folds clean linen in a walnut box, an American plane has taken off shakily from a crowded airstrip on a small Pacific island. It is flying straight towards the rising sun, and the people who try to make it out as it disappears into the distance have to shield their eyes against the fierce glare of the new day. Even the priest who blessed the plane and who is wearing very dark glasses has to strain so much that his eyes are beginning to stream.

Miss Yoshiyuki is busy preparing her class for Confirmation. She has good reason to be pleased with their progress; they have covered great ground in a matter of weeks.

'What is grace?' she says to the twenty-eight girls who are seated at their desks in front of her.

And the twenty-eight girls respond: 'Grace is a supernatural gift bestowed upon us by our loving Creator.'

'How may we receive grace?'

'We receive grace through the Sacraments instituted by Christ.'

'Well,' says Miss Yoshiyuki, 'That's quite an improvement on last week's effort. Fr Dietrich will be very proud of you. He'll have to ask you the hardest questions at the very end of the Catechism, and leave the simpler ones at the start for the weaker class. So perhaps we ought to look again at four hundred to four-eighty.'

The twenty-eight girls make various faces. They are too young to care greatly about such abstruse subjects as Extreme Unction or the Last Judgment.

'Repetition,' says Miss Yoshiyuki. 'Repetition is the key to success. How often must I say it? Now let's begin with the questions about the rewards of the blessed and the punishment of the damned; then we'll revise the three questions about the Apocalypse and the Elect. Fr Dietrich tells me the Bishop has a bee in his bonnet about those ones.'

The class titters, and Miss Yoshiyuki lets them. How could anyone fail to be in wonderful form on such a splendid day? Especially Miss Yoshiyuki, who is wearing an orchid given her by a secret admirer whom the class is determined to identify as Saburo Tanikazi, the gym instructor with the gammy leg.

When the tittering has stopped, Miss Yoshiyuki resumes.

'Close your Catechisms, please, and turn them face downward on the desks. Yumiko, I can't imagine why you're still grinning, but I can guess. Now sit straight and face front. Miyako, I think you could open the window. It's very warm today. Just a little.'

And the lavish sounds of the late summer, deft and delicate, circulate in the classroom: insects and birdsong, the light scuff of sandals on gravel, the low patter of a watering-can as it shifts among the rose-beds.

'That's perfect,' says Miss Yoshiyuki. 'Good girls. All together now – that is, as soon as Maki has returned to us from dreamland. Good. So. How are the blessed rewarded in Heaven?'

'The blessed in Heaven shall see God face to face.'

'Good. Though I'm not sure I saw your lips moving, Komako. Don't be shy or I may make the mistake of thinking that you don't know.'

And there are more titters, the lovely sanity of laughter.

'Quiet please. Now. A simple one. What are angels?'

It is her favourite question; she was asked it herself at her own confirmation fifteen years before, and her heart had hammered as she stuttered the answer.

But the twenty-eight students have it off pat.

'Angels are pure spirits created by God to love and worship Him.'

The schoolroom where Miss Yoshiyuki is teaching her pupils is part of the German Convent in the city of Nagasaki. It is a spacious, intimate room overlooking a park where no leaves have yet fallen, and the park-keeper passes his time by raking the gravel in subtle, concentric circles that are beautiful to examine from the height of three storeys. Otherwise, the poor man sits without moving among the maple trees, and lets his cigarette burn down to the butt before lifting it from his lips with his good arm. The girls at the Catholic convent school think he is mad; Miss Yoshiyuki knows he was driven there. Only a good man could cast such a clean, definite shadow whether he stands or sits. So she shares her egg ration with him each week; in return, he gives her a portion of his sugar allowance. They are the best of friends.

The plane is approaching. It is twelve noon.

The children you heard being called by name are Yumiko, Maki, Komako and Miyako. They are twelve years of age, the daughters of Christian converts. Of the four, three have brothers who went to the war; of the three, two have a brother who cannot come home. When the news was brought to them, each was made to feel quite special in school, and the teachers spoke differently as they passed in the corridor. Even when they idle in the library now, months later, reading a romance instead of reference works, Miss Yoshiyuki strokes the tops of their heads although once she would have tweaked their pigtails sharply. But none of this is of any help at all when they go home again in the late afternoon to find that every room in their respective houses is awash with their brothers' absence, and the tiniest details, like hairs in the soap or a stain in the carpet, can summon them up and in.

I would prefer to have them speak to you in their own voices about these matters and about much else besides, but the dead make a habit of silence, though I think that they listen intently. Were those twenty-eight students to have listened as hard after their lunch-break on August the ninth, they might hear an airplane approaching. They might hear the water tremble in the glass on the stone sill of the classroom window, or the leaves of the geranium quiver minutely under that ugly portrait of the tight-lipped Italian foundress.

But they are occupied, and preoccupied. In a little while, they are to be confirmed. The heavens will open above them, Fr Dietrich has said, and the gifts of the Holy Spirit will rain down upon them in the form of tongues of fire. They must brace themselves for that moment.

'And you will be soldiers of Christ! Or perhaps not soldiers, hmm?' Fr Dietrich chuckles, and the whole class chuckles with him. This is not because they see the point of the joke, but because they are each and every one of them so fond of this big and bearlike priest whose stomach rumbles at morning mass and whose soutane has a shiny bottom from the saddle of the bicycle he rides to and fro among his parishioners. 'No, not soldiers,' Fr Dietrich muses. 'Perhaps we have too many of them already, no? Well, if not soldiers, ambulance drivers. Or stretcher-bearers, yes? The stretcher-bearers of the Lord. How about that? Orderlies, nurses, attendants. Noble work.'

The girls are grinning openly. Miss Yoshiyuki is afraid she may be losing control; and she prides herself on her discipline.

'Miyako,' she calls, in that curious habit we have of singling out one where all are at fault. 'Miyako, will you please pay attention to what Fr Dietrich is saying? And leave the wasp alone. If you don't bother it, it won't bother you.'

Fr Dietrich is undecided about this.

'I wonder is that wise?'

'What, Father?'

'The wasp. I will happily turn my cheek to a human hostile, but wasps are, if you will pardon the eccentricity of the expression, a horse of a different colour.'

'I don't follow you, Father.'

'I can hardly follow myself. Mixed metaphors have always been my forte. I mean perhaps that Miyako can pummel the wasp with my priestly approval. The last time I got bitten on my hand, I couldn't type for two days.'

Miss Yoshiyuki hides her impatience. Fr Dietrich is, after

all, a special case. In the early spring of that same year, he had left his bedroom and slept in the corridor so that sparrows could nest above his curtain rail. Allowance had to be made.

'But I must go,' says the burly priest. 'I must try to ring Fr Kleinsorge; I've been trying to get through for two days now. You'd think that Hiroshima had vanished off the face of the earth.'

'And are you happy with them?' asks Miss Yoshiyuki anxiously. 'With the girls, I mean? With their knowledge of the Catechism?'

'They are word perfect. They have all the answers off to a T. Now the only question which remains is one for which no answer exists. A reply perhaps, but no answer.'

Miss Yoshiyuki is puzzled.

'Is it a question of doctrine?'

'No,' says Fr Dietrich. 'It is a question of love.'

The plane is nearer still, almost on target. It is early afternoon.

It is nearly time to leave you but before I do, in the minutes that remain to us, I want to tell you what little I know of the last moments of our Confirmation class. Where to begin is a problem; where to end, especially with an ending such as this, is a mystery.

Maki was at the dentist this morning. She tried very hard not to whimper as he shook the fragments of tooth back and forth until they broke free separately from her swollen gum. The side of her mouth is still numb from the anaesthetic. It feels strange. When she speaks, she slurs. When she bends down, her jaw aches. So she sits bolt upright and holds a damp napkin against her cheek. When the wound throbs, she offers it up for her brother aboard an aircraft carrier a thousand miles south of Japan.

Komako is thinking about her father, Mr Toraiwa. He works too hard and has difficulty breathing when he gets out of bed or when he laughs too much. She wishes he could find another job away from the depot. Only last night she crept out from between the sheets and walked on tip-toe to his bedroom to listen at the door and make sure he was sleeping and not staring up at the ceiling as if it were the sea or a fire. Perhaps it is best that he never speaks of his wife and his son; on the other hand, perhaps it would be good to do so. Perhaps it would ease his grief. Komako thinks she will talk to Fr Dietrich about this the next time she sees him. He had a way with him; he would understand.

Yumiko and Miyako sit together. Yumiko is colouring an atlas with a pretend empire which stretches from Rangoon to Adelaide. She is about to conquer Indonesia with the colour purple. Then she plans to annex Mexico in a lightning strike.

Miyako scarcely notices her friend. She is in another world, thinking about her boyfriend Yasunari who brought her powdered chocolates two days before. These are pleasant thoughts, and the only thing that disturbs them is her worry over the violin lesson that same morning. The teacher had left her alone for a time, and Miyako had tired of the instrument's weight within minutes. So she laid the violin down on the desk and practised by sawing it like a joint of meat. But the teacher caught her and threatened to inform her parents that their hard-earned supplementary fees were wasted on a most ungrateful girl. Now Miyako is not afraid of her father, Mr Kawabata, because he is deaf in both ears and cares about little other than his budgie, but her mother is another matter, with cross lips and a bony hand.

The plane is overhead. It is the fulness of time.

*

We covered those questions last week. And we revised them several times. I sometimes think that whatever I say to you goes up in smoke, goes in one ear and out the other. Try to remember – if not for my sake, for Fr Dietrich's. What is forgiveness? And what is meant by the sacrament of penance? How did sin enter the world, and how is the world restored to grace again? What happened to the apostles at Pentecost when flame descended upon them? Can none of you tell me? Have none of you a word to say? Are your lips sealed?

    Miyako?

    Yumiko?

    Maki?

    Komako?

    Sometimes I think I might as well be speaking to the dead.

THE LITTLE MERMAN

'*N'AS pas peur, n'as pas peur, n'as pas peur.*'

It was the same last night. The tree, the moon, the beach. Then the room. Hiding in it, in the darkness, waiting. It never changes, you see. Sometimes the sequence is different. Sometimes the beach isn't in it, the moon may be gone. But it always ends in that room, the room we shared. With me waiting. And my hands so cold it hurts to touch myself.

Last night it began with the moon. I could see the earth away in the distance, curled up, blue and white, like a foetus in water. And I heard myself saying, no, shouting, shouting: I will not have this dream. I screamed it, you see, and the glass in my helmet began to fog. I woke up then. I sat up. I listened intently. But the whole ward was sleeping. Even the night nurse was asleep. I could see the mosquitoes round the Anglepoise on the night desk. And my chest was so tender, I couldn't touch them. I lay there, hurting. And the pain calmed me.

If Stephanos was here, he'd say 'N'as pas peur, n'as pas peur.' He always comforted in French. English for banter, French for comfort, German for anger, and Greek for the groceries. Wine and potatoes. Yet it was strange, because in Greek, in his own language, he was lost, a boy, uncertain suddenly, afraid even. As if he knew. Because he must have known, you see, or sensed it. From the time he went to the island, it must have been there; or from before that, from the time he came here to the clinic for the first injections. It must have been there from the start as a kind of rendezvous.

He did know. But I didn't; and it wouldn't have mattered anyway. I could have done nothing; I had nothing to do with it. Because when they asked me, hitting me, in the room, in the darkness, I didn't tell them. I said nothing. And it was too dark to see any of the faces.

I tried to stop him. As soon as I saw what would happen, I tried to. Because the villagers started to blame us, you see. First for the boat and then for the boy. For the Bambakouri boy. And it was nonsense. They said that the boat stopped coming because the passengers wanted donkeys, and white-wash in the streets, and bougainvillaea. Not strange men in kaftans, with highlights in their hair. They said that we'd sickened the tourists, driven them off. But it was nonsense.

And then they found the Bambakouri boy. At the foot of the cliff. If he'd fallen anywhere else. From the cliff at the beach where the ordinary tourists went, where you could buy beer and rent pedalos. But he fell from the cliff where we used to swim and where nobody came. And they blamed us for it. They said we'd been talking to him, leading him on. It was nonsense. And Stephanos said to me: 'It was as if the whole village stood behind the boy, and pushed. He didn't just fall. His blood is on their hands.' Which was true. Because Stephanos thought, and he was right, that the boy's friends had dared him to do it, to creep along the cliff-top and spy on us. To be a scout for them, and report back. To discover, you see, what it was that made their parents so angry, so silent. Because there was a group of children in the village who'd force the smaller ones to dash across the street, touch the door of the Easter Island Club, and dart off again. As if their lives depended on it. And I said to Stephanos: 'If his father had known that the boy was coming to spy on us, he would have beaten him with a length of wet rope.'

He said nothing then. But all night he swore in German. And the next day or the day after, we walked through the village to Nomikou's place, and he wouldn't serve us. Not even drinks, a glass of water. Stephanos wouldn't budge. He was ranting in German. So I had to pull him – not just coax him, but tug him bodily – back to the Club. On our way we met ten, a dozen perhaps, of the boys, none of them dressed in kaftans now, faces scrubbed, subdued. Thierry had gone, Paul had left. Karl was packing, he told us, and leaving tomorrow, with or without Hans.

'Come to Munich,' he said. 'The Easter Island Statues Club can have a second life there. A pocket of Weimar, of old Saint Petersburg, to instil a little frisson into all that *Gemütlichkeit*.'

Karl was uneasy, he kept boxing the air with his fists. But he was right. I said the same thing to Stephanos back in the Club. No lights, a candle, just the two of us. I implored him.

'Listen to me, little merman. Tonight was different. When you lose Nomikou, you've lost the village.'

And Stephanos said: 'Nomikou can go stick it up his daughter,' and something in German.

'But that's the point,' I said to him. 'If a man like Nomikou won't have you in his restaurant, there is no one left.'

He was smoking a Camel. I could tell he was upset. He tipped ash in his Pernod.

'No-one?' he said. Not sadly, not accusingly. And I knew from the way that he held his cardigan closed over his breasts.

'You have me,' I said. Or something. And it frightened me. It frightened me that I shared his room. And it frightened me to remember being with him that day when he pulled off his blouse on the pedalo at the end of the breakwater where the policeman was swimming with his son, and saw us, and covered the boy's eyes with his hand.

And Stephanos said to me then: 'Perhaps we should go to Athens. I have friends in Kolonaki. They live in a huge apartment with cats and tortoises, and the tortoises have their shells painted mauve to go with the carpets. They're a sweet pair. All day they water their poinsettias, and feel ashamed of being wealthy. But they have every possible recording of Clair de Lune, and that makes everything bearable. You'll be happy there.'

His face in the candle-light. Delicate, strong. And I thought of the time he went to the church . . . so I said to him: 'Yes. Come to Athens and I'll play Debussy for you, and talk to you at night when you can't sleep.' He said it was my suavest proposition. And perhaps it was. Because in all that time, more than two years, I'd never felt, you see, so quiet towards him. He kept toying with his glass, and dropping pellets of wax into the candle. No, never so quiet. Not even the first time when he undressed towards me instead of away from me, opening his shirt buttons clumsily, as if he were a string of pearls about to burst open, and go everywhere. Not even then. When he held his hands over them, his doves, his *petites colombes*, like a bashful girl at a public baths, until I said to him, so quietly I couldn't tell whether he heard me: 'They're beautiful.' Or something. The curtains were lifting at the window, and the shadow of the clothes-line bobbed over the bedframe. There was a moment, you see; then it passed. I could hear the village again. And Stephanos became . . . Stephanos. Talkative, pert. Like he was in the Club, where the smoke and the shadows made everything safe for us. Except for that last night. Except for that.

I never dream of them, those moments. They're not tainted, you see, not the least bit harmed by anything that happened before or after. Which is why I can't understand it. The tree, the moon, the beach. Not night after night, of course, but more and more often now. And the beach never happened. I never covered him with sand while he was sleeping. Never trailed sand along his spine the way you see other . . . and the tree, the tree because of where it was. I can understand the tree. I never noticed it, never peed against it, never climbed it, never carved my initials on it. But it was there at least. A eucalyptus. Very old. The bark hanging in strips. Columns of ants going up and down its whitewashed sides, busy about whatever it is that ants are busy about, and sometimes falling off the branches on to the chess-board. And I'd dip my finger in the wine, and make a circle round the ant on the table. He'd go round and round in a frenzy until Stephanos would put his face down, and blow it off.

And the moon. I can understand that. Because he got carried away, you see, by those three American astronauts who were stranded in the Sea of whatever it was called, Tranquillity, Chaos. Even the Pope was praying for them. And Stephanos trotted off to light candles . . . But when they found me in the room, it wasn't the way I dream it. My nose was bleeding. Big drops like black grapes. I couldn't stop it. I tried to hold my head back, and it choked me. Which proves, you see, that the dream is a lie. Because even if I'd wanted to tell them, I couldn't have. I couldn't breathe. And I had warned him. That very same night in the Club when we talked about Athens. After the Bambakouri boy. After Nomikou threw us out. I said to him: 'Little merman, let's go away. Little merman, leave me alone.'

He was a Greek, they said. He was a Cypriot. He was Egyptian. From Smyrna, Cairo, Limassol, Lebanon. And he spoke four languages, they said. But he never spoke, they said. He had a speech impediment. He spoke in riddles. He never stopped talking. He was born, not made. It wasn't chemical, they said, it was surgical. They said it was neither chemical nor surgical, it was genetic.

It went on: the talk, the speculation. I'd been in the town three days, and wherever I went they were talking about him. The children looked at him through their fingers, and their parents walloped them indoors. Women using mangles at their front doors would cross themselves as he passed. The men looked into the middle distance, the priests looked through him, the tourists became intent upon snorkels and beach mats. And the police ... the police looked at his breasts, from beneath the peaks of their hats, revolving the toothpicks in their mouths. And Stephanos would sail by, beaming. Nodding to left and right like a monsignor. Carrying crates of avocados and boxes of wine into the Easter Island Statues Club.

On the fourth day I went there. I sat in an alcove by myself, and watched him dance. Not on the floor, on the tables. And later he served me my wine, poured it out for me, told me to blow on his forehead to cool it, sipped from my glass, said it was ghastly, and brought me no change.

I watched him all night.

The next day I followed him through the town, walking behind him at a little distance, keeping him in sight. From shop to store, from one street to another. All whitewashed, all the same. He walked so quickly I thought I'd lose him. I couldn't keep up. The streets confused me: high, blinding. He'd turn off, disappear. I'd stop, wait, look around, then see him again, behind me now, at a corner. The edge of his shirt, a necklace of melon seeds. Gone. Or he'd stop; I'd wait. Walk on, I'd start again. Blind alleys, culs-de-sac, dead ends. Then a passageway where the houses met over the street, a flash of the sea through a hole in the wall, the noise of gulls bickering over scraps, geckoes slipping like leaves into the shadows, and there, at the end of a lane that led off sharply, a last swerve into the courtyard. The tree, the table, the chess-board. Silence.

'I thought you'd never come. I'd given you up. I kept looking back, but I lost you. I was so disappointed. Won't you play chess with me? Say you will. I know you can. I know a chess-player. And if you make one elegant move, just one, I'll let you win the game. And perhaps the second one too.

'It's so flattering to be followed. It quite made my heart race. I thought only nicotine could do that now. Are you bored? No, don't tell me. I'm sure you're called Georgios, or something quite portly. I may call you . . . David. You have a Davidy something about you. I'm not sure what.

'That was a silly move. Take it back. We shall pretend your finger didn't really leave that pawn. It's rather a nice finger. Your little finger, sad to say, is most unremarkable. But your third finger, your third finger is a joy.

'Take your time. We have all the time in the world. And perhaps we'll be great friends, and I'll worry about you if you go for a swim too soon after lunch. Aha. I see. Not bad. A solid, sensible, Soviet move. My queen is in danger already.'

And the tree shivered in a tiny breeze.

Back in the Club, he turned the lights out and the music on. Allegri's *Miserere* swelled from every speaker.

'Do you mind?' he asked me. 'My only pretension to culture. A little honey sweetens the loaf. Now you must talk to me while I work. And try to finish your sentences. Don't always leave me in suspense. No. Wait a while. Listen . . .'

And I'd watch him rubbing the mirrors with a chamois. Or at times he'd look at himself in a puzzled way, sadly, like a disappointed parent, and he'd say 'Ah, Stephanos, Stephanos.'

His face staring back at him out of the mirror, like the face of a body frozen in ice. As if it knew. As if he knew. And I thought – . . .

'Think, think. You're always thinking. You should wonder instead. Wonder does wonders. The villagers look at me; but look at them. When they're young, they make love in the fields. The rabbits sit back on their haunches and watch with amazement. And they sing the saddest of songs, and bitch about life in the cities. The young men come back from the army, and they kick their sisters from one end of the house to the other; but they mean no harm. And when they're happy, they cry with the pain of it. They want to eat and drink the world, and mop up the spills with a crust of bread. After they marry they get heavy, their shoulders sag, their hearts sink, and the whites of their eyes go out. They wait for death, the way you wait for the doctor. "He'll come," they tell you, "when he's ready." They curse me, it's true. But they curse the sea, and they make their living from it. They curse the heat, but the cold kills them. They curse the island, but the ones who leave it, come back to it to die. You see them up in the graveyard, cutting the grass back on their family plots. Making room.'

And I said to him: 'Little merman, they'll watch an insect on the ground for half an hour because they have nothing better to do. Then somebody calls them, they get up to go. And they stub the ant like a cigarette with their foot.'

'Vous avez tort,' he said to me. 'Vous vous trompez. Courage.'

He was wilful, you see. Incurably Stephanos. And yet I can see how he might have mistaken the signs. Because there were ordinary folk in the village who weren't at all troubled. Nomikou would sit with his feet in a basin of urine, and say: 'Well, whales are warmblooded. And what about flying fish?

Isn't that a contradiction?' And there was Maria, with her faded photos of a drowned son, and no corpse in the grave she kept tidy. And the man with throat cancer who used to play Patience all day long under the awning, and raise both hands to greet everyone. They liked him. They were proud, almost. As if they had a rare, expensive animal no other island could boast of. As if he made up for the lack of ruins, the lack of beaches, the lack of interest. He was that, you see, a kind of dolphin, coming back year after year to the same dirty harbour. They watched for him. So when I had the sense that they were surrounding him, I wasn't sure at first. I couldn't tell that they were ganging up on him, because it seemed instead as if they were closing ranks around him. So I said nothing. And Stephanos went on dancing. Intent upon it. Not on the floor. On the tables. At the window. Always at the window. Shutters thrown wide. Open to the night air, the night sky. Giggling couples, bewildered tourists. The men around Stephanos stamping their feet, faces shining, sweat, oil, After Sun. Like children on day-release from a borstal. Like men recovering the use of their hands after years in bandages. And the man next to me writhed his shoulders, and the wound of a sunburn, not scabbed, still moist, burst like a plum on the blade of his shoulder bone. Because Stephanos was there to lead them, to dance for them, with his male and female body, his little, hurt breasts with the marks healing around them. I was so happy. I should have known from that, from the tenderness I was feeling. Because tenderness belongs to the last stage, to the phase just before the rendez-vous. And it ends with the meeting, and the meeting place.

'In my next life, I want to be . . . Balanchine. Or a church architect. In my spare time, I'll write children's fiction. Unicorns, pumpkins, that sort of thing. Every orphan will get a pair of clogs, and the handsome princes will turn into beautiful kings. And in my third life, in my life after that, I want to stay celibate and devote my time to enlightenment. If I'm tempted, I'll sleep in the freezer. What do I want in my present life? Is that what you said? I'm an unreconstructed exhibitionist. It's a wholetime job. I have obligations to my vices. I need to be loved, but I can't drink milk from myself. If no one will love me, I'll settle for fascination. If I can't even have that, distaste will do. Marriages based on distaste will outlast aluminium. The people we like are of secondary value. What are you saying? Are you of secondary value?'

He said something. He heard me. I saw his lips move. But the music stormed around us, I couldn't hear him. I couldn't hear him. *N'as pas peur, n'as pas peur.* The tree, the moon, the beach. Packing the sand between his legs, where the hairs were wet and sleek. But the beach never happened. So I say to myself, out loud, quite calmly, 'This is a dream. I do not choose to have it.' I turn round, you see, but instead of a street with two doors and a white stone step in front of each of them, I see a moon landscape. Like tundra. My breath starts to cloud. I feel the weight of a helmet on my head. I start to turn, with my arms thrown out wide for balance. Because I'm afraid of being touched. Somebody is about to touch me. The hills and craters swirl faster, faster. English for banter, German for anger, French for comfort. A man lighting a candle for three American astronauts. 'You think too much,' he'd say. Because if I stop, because if I stop. And when they found me, holding me, hitting me, banging my face against the basin, I didn't tell them. 'Where is he?' they said. I couldn't breathe. And it was far too dark to make out any of the faces . . .

When I wake up at night, and the night nurse is asleep, I sit in the bed and I feel my chest paining. The silence seems to be holding its breath. Sometimes the others are awake as well, or sitting out of bed, just staring at their feet. A few of them smoke, looking up at the ceiling, blowing the smoke slowly through their mouths. But no one speaks. Outside, the trees make noises when the wind parts them. Mutterings like startled birds. You can hear the mosquitoes in the garden. I can think then. When it's silent and my chest hurts. Because I don't think it was the Bambakouri boy, and I don't think . . .

'Think, think, think. Stop thinking so much. You look like a baby that needs to be burped. It makes you pout. Wonder instead. Wonder is good for your skin, for your muscle tone. It lifts the forehead, raises the eyebrows, opens the mouth, moistens the eyes, makes everything new again. Wonder. Who designed the thumb? Ingenious. Did the same hand fashion the rainbow and the scorpion? If so, why not? Is God lonely? Why do men become dentists?'

I wanted to say to him: 'Little merman, why did you light a candle for three American astronauts? Why did you learn their names, the names of their children, of their wives?' Because he kept the radio by him, you see, to follow the splashdown. And his eyes filled up. He was far away. I wanted so much to ask him that, there in the Club, the last time. When we talked about Athens. I touched him with the tip of my finger along the side of his cheek, to the hollow below his ear. I could feel the artery pulse against the pressure of the finger. And he said to me: 'What will the people of fair Kolonaki make of me? And how will the Marxist accountants account for my *petites colombes*?' He was cradling himself, as if they were tender. Bruised. Then, quite without warning, he blew out the candle. And we sat in the darkness, saying nothing.

That was all. That was the last night. Stephanos went to the square to be by himself. And I went back to the room. The streets were empty. No moon. No wind. I undressed in the dark. I lay down. Perhaps I slept or almost slept. It makes no difference now.

The next morning, when the policeman came, I was bathing my face with a sponge. He waited while I dressed. He was very quiet. We walked down to the station. And when we passed the Easter Island Statues Club, I didn't look. He brought me to an office, and went away, and I was left alone. At an open window with a view over the harbour. And a cat sitting on the ledge, cleaning itself, looking up every once in a while as if surprised or remembering something. Quietness drifted like blossom over the carpet. I could hear my own heart.

When the policeman came back, he asked me what had happened to my face. Because it was bloated, you see. As if mosquitoes had fed there all night. But I didn't tell him. I didn't say how they stood around me in the room, in the darkness. How I lay in a ball at their feet, and waited. And how for a moment everything stopped, and their boots seemed to magnify. And after that, I lay there all night, with my face pressed into one of his shirts. But I couldn't smell him off it. The blood on my face had hardened like rust. And my hands were so cold I couldn't touch myself. The policeman asked me again. And I told him I'd walked into a wall, or a mirror, or something.

I did what I could. There was no one to help me. Not even Nomikou. And the Mayor's office would send me, you see, to the station, the station to the port authorities' bureau, and the port authorities' bureau back to the Mayor's office, which, when I got there, was closed for the Easter festival. There was an article, a section, small print in the local municipal code, you see, which prohibited the . . . disposal, that was the nub, the disposal of a body outside the limits of the graveyard as . . . constituted by . . . as constituted by . . .

It was such a relief, shadow where no trees grow, to immerse oneself in the business of paperwork, organization, because it meant, you see, that I didn't have to go down those terrible side-streets, stifling passageways, nearer and nearer, almost there now, a square, a table and chairs, a man who lit candles . . . and his *petites colombes*, his doves, his breasts torn off and kicked around like dead fish. I never knew, never suspected, that one man, not heavy, not tall, that one man could leak so much . . . slippy, like grease. Like butter. I kept slipping. On my knees. And I said to him: 'If they'd held you, if they'd hit your teeth against the handle of the tap, you'd have told them too. You would. Tell me you would. Tell me.' But he said nothing. Nothing at all.

There was no wind, but there was a swell. The boat rolled, and I changed the weight in my legs. The pilot stopped the engine. The policeman brought me a form to sign. I had a red pen, but he said No, red was not permitted, and he gave me his own, which was blue with a quite hard nib that punctured the paper and went through to the palm of my other hand. Two men came forward and lifted the sack. They hoisted it onto the side, onto the gunwale, and held it a moment until the swell tilted the boat and the deck swung toward me, and the sack struck the side of the launch like a log. I sat down then because I was dizzy. The boat was picking up speed, heading back toward the harbour. And two water skiers waved to us as they passed, and one of them lifted his leg out of the water while he was waving, but he wobbled and fell. Slowly, as if he were sinking in quicksand, not in water.

Little merman, my chest is hurting. It burns like dry ice. The doctors offer me ointment; they say to me: 'Pain is not a good in itself.' But I keep on refusing. It puzzles them. They don't understand. That I can think better. I know you say I think too much. But you mustn't fret. I eat well, I read the papers, I take an interest in those around me. At night, I listen to the crickets hissing in the shrubbery. The moon comes right to the end of my bed, and stays there. Or it snows on the other side of the ward, where the night desk is. I can think then. I can choose what to think of. A man in a church lighting candles for three American astronauts. The candles gleaming like lava, a yellow terrace of flame. His face as he lit one off the other. The woman who cleaned the place woke up in her booth and crossed herself when she saw him there.

So the candles come first. When I get back. When I'm home again. And after the candles, the Club. The mirrors where the Swedes used to peel off their kaftans and dance by themselves until somebody chose them. The shutters. Lemon. Open to the night air. The doors thrown wide. And music. Because I want to dance for you there, though I haven't your grace, your litheness, your love of Debussy. 'Dance with me,' you said, that last time, in the small hours, as the sun rose or was about to, and our friends had gone down to the break-water to listen to the roosters. 'Dance with me.' Because you didn't care that Nomikou would refuse to have you in his restaurant two days later. 'Dance with me.' Because they hadn't come yet, and your lips had a red ridge from the wine you were drinking, and your teeth were very white. 'Dance with me.' Because the mirrors hadn't been smashed and the shutters hadn't been broken, and no one had pissed on the seats in the alcoves, and no one had defecated on the dance-floor. 'Dance with me. Dance with me. Dance with me.'

Because I have a rendezvous in that place. A meeting. The pain will start easing them. I won't be uncertain. The little marks will have healed. I won't let the sun see them. And just as I followed you that first time, from one street to the other, in the heat and silence of the morning, and you asked me my name, so, in the very same way, when I'm home, you'll follow me there, to a square, a table, a tree. The music will have gone out in the Easter Island Statues Club. And I'll wait then. They'll come when they're ready. And I wonder will I know any of them. It may be too sudden, too dark, noises, feet peltering. But I'll know what you felt, what you heard, what you waited for. I won't have to wonder anymore. Because I do wonder. All the time. And wonder does wonders. For the skin, the complexion. It lifts the forehead, moistens the eyes, quickens the breath, makes everything, everything new again.

GEOFF NICHOLSON

THE KNOT GARDEN

'Nicholson juggles with breathless skill, and an enormous sense of enthusiasm'

The Times

'THE KNOT GARDEN starts with the presumed suicide of TV gardening sage Richard Wisden, whose posthumous biddings propel his wife Libby on a tour of friends and some-times acquaintances to investigate the circumstances of his life and death . . . ingenious . . . earns top marks for originality and puzzlement'

The Literary Review

'An intricate structure of detection and drama'

Daily Telegraph

'A clever young writer playing games'

The Guardian

'Nicholson has fine style, a wonderful eye for character, delightful humour and a lovely insight into life and its more ridiculous moments . . . A novel which you dare not put down until the end'

Eastern Evening News

sceptre

WILLIAM McILVANNEY

WALKING WOUNDED

'A superb collection: a series of brief lives which McIlvanney
passes through the eye of a very sharp needle'
The Literary Review

'In the mythical Ayrshire town of Graithnock the walking
wounded of the title are those excluded from the Scottish
economic "renaissance" – labourers, publicans, greyhound
fanciers, spinsters. The true nature of their lives, McIlvanney
suggests, lies in their dreams . . . Several of these stories
are little more than the random flotsam of public-bar life,
conversations overheard, small cameos observed and etched
in meticulous detail. McIlvanney's great skill lies not only in
illuminating these fleeting events which hint at, or embody
greater truths, but in evoking an entire life within the compass
of a few hundred words . . . His triumph is to find the
consolation of hope in the face of apparently fatalistic despair,
to find poetry in the cadences of common speech, and the inner
sadness of his subjects' lives, while always reaffirming their
fortitude and resilience'
The Sunday Times

'Never depressing, the stories are epics of people in pain,
families at odds . . . He is a master of hilarious melancholy. His
prose has pith and punch'
David Hughes in The Mail on Sunday

'A clear direct style, great charm and good humour'
Financial Times

'McIlvanney's most profound account of selves and their drift
and jeopardies . . . very moving and rather frightening'
New Statesman

Current and forthcoming titles from Sceptre

WILLIAM McILVANNEY

WALKING WOUNDED
THE BIG MAN
DOCHERTY

GEOFF NICHOLSON

THE KNOT GARDEN

MARK OLDHAM

NEW VALUES

LIAM O'FLAHERTY

THE INFORMER

BOOKS OF DISTINCTION